A marriage in name only?

Cassie held out her left hand so Trace could nestle the white-gold wedding band next to the engagement ring he'd given her on the plane to Phoenix. His movements were sure and steady.

She glanced up as the justice of the peace began to speak. ''Now, with the power invested in me by the state of Arizona, I pronounce you husband and wife. It's not part of the official ceremony to kiss the bride, but—''

Trace's head descended and his mouth swiftly covered hers. Cassie hadn't expected more than a chaste kiss; she wasn't prepared for the heady sensation that left her clinging to him, weak and drained.

''Ma-ma! Ma-ma!'' The babies' cries slowly penetrated her consciousness. Cassie broke the kiss, but in the split second before she turned her burning face away, she thought she saw a look of desire in his eyes.

By the time he lifted his head, it was gone, and she decided she'd imagined it.

Dear Reader,

Long before I became a writer, I loved reading Harlequin Romance books. I still prefer them to other types of romance fiction because, to my mind, they embody all the elements for the ideal life: physical, mental and spiritual love between a man and a woman, sacrifice and commitment to marriage and the rearing of children in a home where love reigns and wholesome values are taught.

When I wrote *Both of Them,* I wanted to bring all of these elements together in a novel that I hope will touch your heart. I also wanted to meet the challenge of telling a very "traditional" story in a contemporary way—the marriage-of-convenience story, which remains an enduring favorite with romance readers everywhere.

You can't imagine my delight when my editor told me that *Both of Them* had been chosen as one of the titles in The Bridal Collection. I treasure my association with Harlequin and feel uniquely blessed by this opportunity.

I'd also like to express my gratitude to you, the reader. It is *for* you and *because* of you that I write. I know we share many of the same ideas about the importance of love—and the importance of *stories* about love. And I hope my books reflect your beliefs, as they do mine, and entertain you with a few hours of reading pleasure.

I'm deeply honored that you've made me part of your life.

With thanks,

Rebecca Winters

BOTH OF THEM
Rebecca Winters

Harlequin Books

TORONTO • NEW YORK • LONDON
AMSTERDAM • PARIS • SYDNEY • HAMBURG
STOCKHOLM • ATHENS • TOKYO • MILAN
MADRID • WARSAW • BUDAPEST • AUCKLAND

ISBN 0-373-03210-2

Harlequin Romance first edition July 1992

BOTH OF THEM

CHAPTER ONE

HE WAS THE BABY'S FATHER all right! The same olive complexion, the familiar obstinate chin, the identical hair, black as India ink. Even from the distance separating them, the resemblance seemed to shout at Cassie.

She leaned against the doorjamb in disbelief. Her sister's motherly intuition hadn't failed her, after all.

Cassie, from the first moment I held Jason in my arms, I thought there was something...different about him. If Ted was still alive, he'd say the same thing. Jason's not our son! I'm convinced of it!

Remember I told you how he was rushed to the intensive-care unit as soon as he was born? And remember my telling you about a disaster that brought all those victims to the hospital at the same time? There was so much commotion that morning, I honestly think a mix-up occurred and they brought me back the wrong baby from intensive care.

Jason belongs with his natural parents. Promise me you'll find my baby and take care of him for me, Cassie. Then I can die in peace.

Faced with the irrefutable proof of Jason's true paternity, Cassie went alternately hot and cold. Down to the smallest detail, like the shape of the long, square-tipped fingers, or the way one dark brow lowered with displeasure, nine-month-old Jason was the robust replica of Trace Ellingsworth Ramsey III, the autocratic male she could see through the doorway seated behind the desk. He was rapping out edicts over the phone to some no doubt terrified underling of the Greater Phoenix Banking Corporation.

Her eyes closed in reaction, because it meant Susan's natural son had left the hospital with this prominent, high-powered banking executive and his wife. Susan's baby would now have the Ramsey name, would now be assured his place in life as one of the Ramsey heirs.

Had the Ramseys, like Susan, ever wondered about that day nine months ago? Had they ever sensed anything about their baby that didn't seem right? Any physical characteristics, for instance, that didn't appear in their families?

"Come in, Miss Arnold!" Trace Ramsey called out, not bothering to hide his impatience as he put down the receiver. Before entering the room Cassie darted a nervous glance at Jason, who was still asleep in his carryall next to the secretary's desk.

Though high heels added several inches to her five-foot-three-inch frame, Cassie felt dwarfed by the dimensions of the walnut-paneled office. To her disappointment there were no mementos or framed photographs of Ramsey's wife and son. Except for some paintings on the walls and a bonsai tree placed on a corner of his desk, the suite was immaculate, and blessedly cool.

She sat down in one of the chairs opposite his desk. "Thank you for taking time out of your busy schedule to see me this morning, Mr. Ramsey. I realize it was short notice."

His dark brows furrowed in undisguised irritation. "According to my secretary, Mrs. Blakesley, you have a highly confidential matter to discuss with me, which you refused to disclose to her."

"I couldn't say anything to her," Cassie said immediately, her guileless, leaf-green eyes pleading with him to believe her. "It's no one's business but ours. When I say ours, I'm including your wife, of course," she added in a soft voice.

He sat forward in the chair with his hands clasped on top of the desk, gazing directly at Cassie. She stared into his eyes, deep blue eyes set between impossibly black lashes. Like Jason's... The Ramsey eyes reminded Cassie of the intense blue in a match flame.

"My secretary never arranges appointments without first obtaining background information, Miss Arnold. She made an exception in your case. I hope for your sake you were telling her the truth when you said this was a life-and-death situation. Lying to gain entry to my private office is the surest way to find yourself slapped with a lawsuit for harassment. As it is, I'm taking time from an important board meeting to accommodate you."

His arrogance took her breath away. If all this weren't for the ultimate happiness of everyone concerned, she would've relished storming out of there and slamming the door in his good-looking face.

"This concerns your son," she said quietly.

The menacing look that transformed his taut features made her heart leap in apprehension. With dangerous agility, he got up from his seat and placed both hands on his desk, leaning forward. "If you're part of a kidnapping scheme, let me warn you I've already activated the security alarm. When you walk out of here, it'll be with an armed guard."

"Are you always this paranoid?" She was aghast; until now it hadn't occurred to her that his wealth made him a target for kidnappers. At the mere thought, a shudder ran through her body.

"You've got thirty seconds to explain yourself." The implicit threat in his voice unnerved her.

"I-I think you'd better sit down," she said.

"Your time is running out."

In an attempt to feel less vulnerable, Cassie rose to her feet, clutching her purse in front of her. "It's not easy for me to explain when you're standing there like . . . like an avenging prince ready to do battle."

He flicked a glance at his watch. "You're down to ten seconds. Then you can explain all this to a judge." From the forbidding expression on his face and the coldness of his voice, she knew he meant what he said.

As worried and nervous as she was about confronting him with the truth, she had to remember that this man and his wife were her only passport to Susan's son. That knowledge gave her the courage to follow through with her plan.

Taking a deep breath, she said, "I happen to know that you and your wife have a nine-month-old baby boy who was born to you on February twenty-fourth at the Palms Oasis Health Center. My sister, Susan Arnold Fisher, also delivered a baby boy there on the same day.

"Until the moment she died, she believed that there was an upset in routine because of the catastrophe—the chemical plant explosion. It brought a flood of injured people to the hospital, and somehow the wrong name tags were put on the babies' wrists in the intensive-care unit. The result was that my sister was presented with your baby, and you and your wife went home with hers."

The silence following her pronouncement stretched endlessly. His face looked impassive, hard and cold as stone. "All right," he finally muttered. "I've listened to your tale. Now I hope you have a good attorney, because you're going to need one."

"Wait!" she cried when he pressed the intercom button. She had expected this encounter to disturb him, but she'd never dreamed he would call in the authorities before she had convinced him of the truth!

"It's too late to backtrack, Miss Arnold."

A knock on the door brought Cassie's head around and she saw an armed security guard and a police officer enter the room with their hands on their unsnapped holsters. Behind them stood an anxious Mrs. Blakesley. She held a wriggling, squirming Jason, who was bellowing at the top of his lungs.

"What in the—?" Trace Ramsey stopped midsentence and raked a hand through his black hair, shooting Cassie a venomous glance. But she was too concerned to be intimidated; dropping her purse, she made a beeline for Jason.

Since Susan's death two months earlier, Cassie and Jason had become inseparable. She might not have been his biological mother, but she loved him every bit as fiercely. She felt guilty for leaving him in Mrs. Blakesley's care, even for such a brief time. He must have awakened after his morning bottle and been frightened by the unfamiliar face hovering over him.

"What's the trouble, Mr. Ramsey?" asked the guard. But Cassie didn't hear his answer, because Jason had caught sight of her. Immediately his lusty cries intensified, resounding through the suite of offices. "Ma-ma, Ma-ma," he repeated, holding out his hands.

Despite the gravity of the situation, Cassie couldn't repress a tiny smile, because it was Trace Ramsey's own noisy son creating all this chaos.

"Mommy's here, darling." With a murmured thank-you, she plucked him from the older woman's arms and cuddled him against her chest, kissing his damp black curls, rubbing his strong sturdy little back with her free hand.

Jason had made it clear that he wanted Cassie and no one else. He clung tightly to her and calmed down at once. Cassie felt a wave of maternal pride so intense she was staggered, and at that moment she knew she could never give him up. She knew she'd made a mistake in coming here.

With the best of intentions, Cassie had walked into Trace Ramsey's office and upset his comfortable, well-ordered life. If his reaction to a possible kidnapping attempt was anything to go by, his love for the son he'd brought home from the hospital was as great as hers for Jason. She wanted to honor her sister's dying wish, but she *couldn't*. She realized that now. It was wrong, unfair—to all of them.

"Mr. Ramsey?" she started to say, but the second she caught sight of his ashen face, the name died on her lips. In her preoccupation with Jason's needs, she hadn't noticed that everyone except his father had left the room. He stood motionless in its center.

Swallowing hard, she loosened Jason's fist, which was clutching her hair, before turning him around to face his father. Only seconds later, she heard his shaken whisper. "Dear Lord, the likeness is unbelievable."

Cassie's compassionate heart went out to him. She couldn't imagine what it would feel like to learn that she'd been nurturing the wrong child since his birth, let alone to see her own baby for the first time.

"That was my reaction as soon as I saw you," she said quietly. He looked away from the child then, and gazed at her, his eyes dark with emotion.

"He's called Jason," Cassie added. The sound of his name brought the baby's dark head around and he clamored to be held in his favorite position, with his face buried in her neck, his hand gripping the top of her dress for dear life.

"May I hold him?" Trace's voice sounded strained. He lifted his hands instinctively to take Jason from her.

"Yes, of course. But don't be surprised if he starts crying again. He's going through that stage where he won't let anyone near him but me."

Jason immediately protested the abrupt departure from Cassie's arms. His strong little body squirmed and struggled, and he kicked out his legs, screaming loudly enough to alert the entire building. But not for anything in the world would Cassie have intruded on this private moment between father and son.

They looked so right together, so perfect, it brought a lump to her throat.

Trace's gaze swerved to hers as he bounced his unhappy son against his broad shoulder, apparently unconcerned about his elegant, stone-gray silk suit. "Do you have a bottle I can give him? Maybe it'll quiet him down."

She should have thought of that. She began to rummage in the bag Mrs. Blakesley had brought in. "Here."

Gently but firmly he settled Jason in his arm and inserted the nipple in his mouth. He performed the maneuver with an expertise that would have surprised her if she hadn't known he'd been fathering Susan's son for the past nine months.

But Jason wasn't cooperating. He just cried harder, fighting the bottle and his father with all his considerable might. Cassie could tell that Trace was beginning to feel at a loss.

"Why don't you let me change him?" she suggested softly. "It might do the trick."

He slanted her a look she couldn't decipher and with obvious reluctance put a screaming Jason back in her arms. While Jason snuggled against her once more, his father reached for the baby quilt lining the carryall and spread it on top of his desk, pushing the telephone aside. Never had she imagined she'd be changing Jason's diaper there!

"Come on, sweetheart. Mommy's going to make you comfortable." Though Jason continued to protest vociferously and eye his father as if he were the enemy, she managed to make him lie still long enough to unfasten his sleeper and peel it off along with his damp diaper.

As she put on a clean disposable diaper, Trace murmured something unintelligible beneath his breath, and almost as if he couldn't help himself took Jason's right foot in his hands. For some reason the baby didn't seem to mind and actually relaxed a little, no doubt because he was receiving so much attention. His extremities had become of paramount importance in his young life.

Cassie had always been intrigued by Jason's right foot. The third and fourth toes were webbed, a characteristic never seen in either Susan's or Ted's families. His father seemed to find it of inordinate interest, as well.

"He's my son!" Trace proclaimed solemnly, then let out a cry of pure delight. Fierce pride gleamed in his blue eyes.

"We probably ought to take the babies to the hospital and have their blood types checked against the records."

"We will," he muttered, "but the truth is sitting right here." He grasped Jason's fingers and pulled experimentally to test the baby's strength. Jason caught hold with a firm grip and lifted his head and shoulders from the desk to sit up without help, producing a satisfied chuckle from his father. Jason had become equally curious about the black-haired stranger who seemed to take such pleasure in playing with him.

Because it was cool in the room, Cassie searched for a clean sleeper in the diaper bag. No sooner had she found one than it was taken from her hands.

"I'll dress him," Trace stated. There was an unmistakable ring of possession in his tone as he proceeded to fit Jason's compact body into the arms and feet of the little white suit.

After snapping the front fasteners, he picked up his son, who had by now stopped fussing, and held him against his shoulder, running his fingers through Jason's wild black curls. Cassie noted that even their hair seemed to part naturally on the same side.

Needless to say, she'd been forgotten as Trace carried Jason over to the window where the great city of Phoenix lay sprawled before them. Whatever he said was for his son's ears alone. She knew that Trace Ramsey had already taken Jason to his heart.

Now there were two people in the world who loved Jason intensely. And as soon as his wife was informed, there would be three. Everything had suddenly become much more complicated. Cassie understood instinctively that Jason's father wouldn't give up anything that was his. But in this case they would have to work out vacation schedules, because she wasn't prepared to lose Jason. She had come to love him too much.

"Mr. Ramsey? I have a plane to catch later today. Do you think we could meet with your wife this morning and tell her what's happened? I can hardly wait to see my nephew, and I'd like some time with him before I go back to San Francisco with Jason."

"San Francisco?" He wheeled around, a grimace marring his features.

"We live there, Jason and I."

Her voice must have attracted Jason's attention because he cried out and reached for her again. When Trace continued to hold him, Jason wailed piteously and tried to wriggle out of his father's grasp. He had been a determined, headstrong child from birth. Now she knew why.

"It's time for his lunch, but a bottle will have to do." The gentle reminder forced Trace to close the distance between them and deposit Jason in her arms. But with every step he took, she could tell he rebelled against the idea of relinquishing his newly discovered son even for a moment.

Cassie couldn't blame him. The situation was so emotionally charged she was afraid she would burst into tears any second. Comforted by the familiar feel of Jason's warm little body, she sat down in a leather wing chair Trace positioned for her. Jason grabbed the bottle with both hands and started gulping down his milk.

Actually he'd been attempting to drink from a cup for the past week. But her pediatrician had said to use a bottle while they were traveling because it would give him a greater sense of security. Jason was such a noisy drinker, Cassie couldn't help smiling and felt Trace's eyes on both of them.

"My wife and I divorced soon after the baby was born," he said abruptly. He paused, then went on, speaking quickly. "She gave me custody and went back to her law practice in Los Angeles. I have my housekeeper, Nattie, to help raise my son. She and her husband, Mike—who looks after the grounds—have worked for me for years. Nattie's wonderful with children, and Justin adores her."

"Justin!" As she said his name, her mind grappled with the unexpected revelation that Mrs. Ramsey was no longer a part of this family's life. She lifted her head and fixed imploring green eyes on Trace. "Tell me about Susan's son—your son," she amended self-consciously. "What does he look like? I-I can't wait to see him."

Without hesitation he strode swiftly to his desk and buzzed his secretary. "Mrs. Blakesley? Cancel all my appointments for today. I'm going home and won't be back. Tell Robert to have my car waiting in the rear. We'll be down shortly. If there are any urgent phone messages, give them to me now."

While he dealt with last-minute business, she felt his gaze linger on her slender legs beneath the cream cotton suit she was wearing. Cassie's heart did a funny little kick, and she forced herself to look away, studying the paintings hung on the walls of his office. Until now, Trace Ramsey had been the focal point of her attention.

If the decor was a reflection of his personal taste, he tended to enjoy the watercolors of an artist unknown to her. The paintings depicted a variety of enchanting desert scenes, in a style that was at once vibrant and restrained. She would have liked one for herself.

A loud burp from Jason brought her back to the present. Trace's spontaneous laugh made him look, for a moment, more carefree, and Cassie chuckled, too. Obviously Jason had finished his bottle without stopping for breath.

"Shall we?" Trace stood at the door holding a briefcase and the carryall, indicating she should join him.

"That's a beautiful boy you have there," Mrs. Blakesley commented to Cassie as they passed her desk on their way out.

"Mrs. Blakesley," Trace said to the older woman, his eyes still glowing in wonder, "I'd like you to be the first person to meet my son, Jason. When I'm in possession of all the facts, I'll explain how this came

about, but for the time being I must ask you to keep
it to yourself.''

"I knew it!" The matronly woman jumped to her
feet. Hurrying around her desk she shaped Jason's
face with her hands. "Even before she said it was a
matter of life and death, I knew it. He bears an amaz-
ing resemblance to you, Trace. I never saw anything
like it in my life!"

A satisfied smile lifted the corners of Trace's mouth
as he gazed down on his son.

Cassie could imagine all too easily what his secretary was thinking—that at one time Cassie and Trace
had had an affair and Jason was the result. She wanted
to set the matter straight, but Trace was already
whisking her out of his office and around the corner
to a private elevator.

When he'd ushered her inside and the doors were
closed, he asked, "How did you get to my office?"

"A taxi."

"How long have you been in Phoenix?"

Jason's curious eyes darted back and forth as they
spoke.

"Only two days this time."

"This time?" His black brow lifted in query. The
elevator arrived at the ground floor and they stepped
out, but Trace remained standing in the hallway as he
waited for Cassie's answer.

"I've made several rushed trips to Phoenix in the
past two months trying to find out if Susan was right
about the switch. There were five couples who'd had

a son at that hospital the same day Susan gave birth to Jason. I mean Justin.''

Trace blinked. ''I didn't realize there were that many. Palms Oasis is a small hospital.''

''I know. I was surprised, too. Anyway, I visited each family in turn but came to a dead end each time. I began to think Jason was one of those rare accidents of nature, after all—the odd gene producing a throwback in the family. That is, until I saw you.'' She ventured a look into his eyes and wondered why she'd ever thought them glacial. ''When your secretary told me you wouldn't see me without knowing the reason for my visit, I almost turned around and walked out.''

His eyes turned an inky blue color and he sucked in his breath. ''Thank God you didn't.''

She gave a quick half smile. ''You're not exactly an easy man to reach, Mr. Ramsey. No home phone. Security guards. I didn't have a choice except to meet you without an appointment. You'll never know how close I came to giving up. You were the last person on my list and it seemed like an unnecessary gesture, another exercise in futility.''

''What made you so persistent?'' he asked soberly.

''I have to admit that since I started looking after Jason, I've entertained some doubts about his parentage, too. I made up my mind to be as thorough as possible, so there'd be no lingering shadows when I returned to San Francisco to raise Jason as my son.''

On impulse she lowered her head to kiss the child's smooth cheek. ''And something told me that if I left without seeing you, I would always have these doubts...."

Just as she spoke, Trace moved closer. He cupped her elbow and guided her through the hall to a back door. A BMW sedan stood waiting in the drive. "Come here, Tiger," he said to Jason, lifting him from Cassie's arms and strapping him in the baby seat.

Jason took one look at the unfamiliar surroundings and began to scream.

"I think I'd better stay with him or you won't be able to concentrate on your driving." She climbed in back, then handed Jason one of his favorite toys, a hard plastic doughnut in bright orange. That calmed him and he soon grew absorbed in chewing it.

Trace leaned inside to fasten her seat belt. His action brought their faces within an inch of each other, and she was painfully conscious of his dark glossy hair, his clean-shaven jaw and his fresh scent—the soap he used? To mask her awareness of him, she pretended to adjust Jason's seat belt. Trace backed away from her and closed the door. In seconds he had gone around to the driver's seat.

"Thanks, Robert," he called to the garage attendant, and they were off. If the older man found the situation somewhat unusual, he didn't let on. But she could tell he was curious about Trace's little black-haired look-alike sitting in Justin's usual spot.

Despite the way he had treated her earlier, Cassie found herself warming to Trace. She liked the fact that he took his fatherhood role so seriously. And she liked the way he accepted a child's presence in his life, not worrying about his costly suit or his expensive car. She knew a lot of men who never allowed children inside their luxury cars.

They left the busy downtown center and drove north toward the foothills, where she could see Camelback Mountain in the distance. What impressed Cassie most about Phoenix was the cleanliness of its streets and the beauty of the residential lawns and gardens. The vivid flowers and shrubs, the sparkling blue of swimming pools...

This was the first time in months that she'd been able to appreciate her surroundings. The pain of her broken engagement, plus the trauma of trying to cope with Susan's death and Jason's needs—on top of running her home handicrafts business—had drained her. She couldn't remember when she'd been able to relax like this.

But her pleasure was short-lived. When she turned her head to find another toy in her bag, she discovered a pair of narrowed eyes watching her through the rearview mirror. If their guarded expression and his taut facial features were any indication, something unpleasant was going through Trace Ramsey's mind. She couldn't understand it, because only moments before everything had been so amicable.

Inexplicably hurt by his oddly hostile look, she closed her eyes and rested her head against the leather upholstery.

In fairness to him, she supposed, it wasn't every day a man kissed the child he thought was his son goodbye, only to be confronted with his *real* son a few hours later.

Again Cassie tried to imagine his feelings and couldn't. Only once in her twenty-five years had she heard of a case involving a switched baby. That instance, too, had been a mischance, sending two families home with each other's babies. Cassie didn't know the statistics, but figured such an accident had to be in the one-in-a-billion category.

Until now, most of Cassie's thoughts and concerns had been for Jason. But the closer they drew to Trace's home, the more excitedly she began to anticipate her first look at Justin. She found herself speculating on why the Ramsey marriage had fallen apart so soon after the baby was born. How could his wife have left her child and gone to another state to pursue a career? Didn't her heart ache for her son?

Cassie couldn't fathom any of it. She was so deep in thought she didn't realize the car had left the highway and turned onto a private road. It wound through a natural desert setting, dotted with saguaros and other cacti, to a breathtaking Southwestern house—a house that looked as if it had sprung from the very landscape.

The house appeared to be built on two levels, with a whitewashed stone exterior and pale wood trim.

The architect who had designed Trace Ramsey's home had not only succeeded in reflecting the environment but had caught the essence of the man. The clean yet dramatic lines, the soaring windows, the quiet beauty of the wood, created a uniquely satisfying effect.

He continued driving around the house to a side entrance where Cassie caught sight of a rectangular swimming pool. Immaculate, velvety green lawns flanked the water, which was as blue as a deep-sea grotto.

Cassie gasped at the sheer size and beauty of Trace Ramsey's retreat, tucked only minutes away from the center of his banking empire. Cassie had never seen anything quite like this place. She'd spent the whole of her life in San Francisco, living with her widowed mother and sister in the bottom apartment of a flat-fronted Victorian house on Telegraph Hill. Cassie couldn't remember her father, who'd died when she was very young.

While she lifted Jason from his car seat, Trace came around and opened the door to assist them. The air smelled of tantalizing desert scents and was fresher than in downtown Phoenix. Cassie thrived in cooler temperatures; she estimated that it couldn't be much warmer than seventy-five degrees. Perfect weather for early December, just the way she liked it.

"Shall we go in?" He didn't seem to expect an answer as he gripped her elbow and helped her up the stairs to the entry hall, carrying the baby bag in his other hand. He didn't attempt to take his son from her, probably because he didn't relish a repeat of Jason's tears. But she could sense Trace's impatience to hold him.

Jason was fascinated by the click of her high heels on the Mexican-tile floors and kept turning his head in an attempt to discover the source. It was a fight to keep him from flipping out of her arms, especially since Cassie found herself so distracted by the beauty around her. Every few steps, she had to stop and stare at the dramatically cut-out white interior walls and bleached wood ceilings.

They walked along a gallery filled with lushly green trees and local Indian art. It looked out on the swimming pool, part of which was protected by the overhanging roof.

"Nattie? I'm home, and I've brought someone with me for lunch. Where are you?" Trace called out as they went down a half flight of stairs toward the indoor portion of the patio.

"Justin's been helping me water the plants. I didn't know you'd be back to eat. I'll get something on the table right away."

They entered a charming courtyard reminiscent of old Mexico, with a profusion of plants and colorful flowers. But Cassie hardly noticed the wrought-iron lounge furniture or the retreating back of the auburn-haired housekeeper. Her eyes fastened helplessly on the child in the playpen who had heard his father's voice and was squealing in delight.

The slender lanky child, dressed in a sleeveless yellow romper suit, was standing, a feat Jason hadn't yet mastered, as he clung to the playpen webbing, rocking in and out as he watched his father's approach.

Round hazel eyes shone from a fringe of fine, straight, pale-gold hair that encircled his head like a halo. His total attention was fixed rapturously on Trace.

Cassie came to a standstill. It was an astonishing sensation—a little like putting the final pieces in a jigsaw puzzle. The frame of this child's body was Ted's, but his complexion was Susan's. The shape of his eyes was Ted's, but the color was Susan's. The texture of the hair was Ted's, but again, the coloring was Susan's. The straight nose and cheekbones were Ted's, but the smile...

Cassie's eyes filled with tears. Her adored sister, who only eight weeks before had lost a valiantly fought battle with pneumonia, lived in her son's glorious smile.

"Oh, Susan!" She sobbed her sister's name aloud and buried her face in Jason's chest. She was overcome with emotion, with feelings still so close to the surface that she couldn't contain them any longer.

Jason fretted, patting her head agitatedly. Cassie fought for control and after a few minutes lifted her tear-drenched face to discover a pair of angry blue eyes staring at her, not only in silent accusation but contempt.

"What's wrong?" she whispered, attempting to wipe the tears from her cheeks. "First in the car, and now here. Why are you looking at me like that?"

CHAPTER TWO

IN THE SILENCE that followed, he reached for Justin and hugged him protectively, rubbing his chin against the fine silk of the child's hair. "I was counting on that reaction and you didn't disappoint me," he said bitterly.

They faced each other like adversaries. Cassie shifted Jason to her other arm. *"What reaction?"* She couldn't imagine what had caused such hostility.

"It's too late for pretense. Justin needs people around who see him for the wonderful person he is."

She shook her head in total bewilderment. "He *is* wonderful!"

"But—"

"But what?" she demanded angrily, feeling a wave of heat wash over her neck and cheeks. Jason could sense the charged atmosphere and started to whimper.

"You're no different from my ex-wife! She was so repulsed by Justin's deformity, mild though it is, that she wouldn't even hold him."

Deformity? "I don't know what you're talking about! Two months ago I watched my sister's body laid to rest and I thought her lost to me for the rest of my life.'' Her voice shook, but she hardly noticed.

Without conscious thought she lowered Jason into the playpen and reached for her tote bag. Oblivious to his sudden outburst, she pulled one of Susan's wedding pictures from the side pocket and held it up for Trace's scrutiny. It was her favorite picture of Susan and Ted, smiling into the camera just before they left on their honeymoon.

"When Justin's face lighted up just now, it was as if God had given Susan back to me. Take a good look at the picture, Mr. Ramsey. See for yourself!"

Grim-faced, he set Justin in the other corner of the playpen and took the photograph. Immediately Justin, too, began to cry. In an effort to distract the howling infants, Cassie knelt beside the playpen and started to sing "Teensy Weensy Spider," one of Jason's favorite songs. Within seconds, both babies grew quiet. Jason crawled toward her, while Justin clambered to his feet.

It was when he put out his left hand to grasp the playpen's webbing that she noticed the depression— like a band around the middle of his upper arm. Below the depression, his arm and hand were correctly shaped, but hadn't grown in proportion to the rest of his body. The deformity was slight, but it was noticeable if you were aware of it.

"You dear little thing." Unable to resist, she stood up and leaned over to take Justin in her arms. "You precious little boy," she crooned against his soft cheek, rocking him gently back and forth.

"Your mother and daddy would have given anything in the world to hold you like this. Do you know that?" she asked as he stared quietly at her. The seriousness of his gaze reminded her of the way Ted used to look when he was concentrating. "Susan made me promise to find you. I'm so thankful I did. I love you, Justin. I love you," she whispered, but the words came out a muffled sob.

She wanted to believe the baby understood when she felt his muscles relax and his blond head rest on her shoulder. For a few minutes Cassie was conscious of nothing but the warmth of her nephew's body cuddled against her own.

"I owe you an apology."

Cassie opened her eyes and discovered Trace standing not two feet from her, with Jason riding his shoulders. His sturdy little fingers were fastened in his father's black hair, a look of fear mingled with intense concentration on his expressive face.

She smiled through the tears. "He's never seen the world from that altitude before."

Miraculously Trace smiled back, their enmity apparently forgotten. Cassie's heartbeat accelerated as she found herself examining the laugh lines around his mouth and his beautiful, straight white teeth. She raised her eyes to his, and the pounding of her heart actually became painful.

"Trace?" the housekeeper called out just then, jerking Cassie back to reality. "Do you want lunch served on the patio or in the dining room?"

"The patio will be fine, Nattie." To Cassie he said, "I'll get the high chair. The boys can take turns having lunch."

The boys. Those words fell so naturally from his lips. Anyone listening would have assumed this was an everyday occurrence.

"Since Jason and I will have to leave for the airport pretty soon, I'd like to spend this time with Justin. Do you mind if I hold him on my lap to feed him?"

A scowl marred his features. "When's your flight?" he demanded, not answering her question.

"Ten after four."

"I'll get you to the airport on time," was the terse response. "Right now the only matter of importance is getting better acquainted." He grasped Jason's hands more tightly. "Come on, Tiger. We'll go get Justin's chair and surprise Nattie."

Jason forgot to cry because he was concentrating all his energy on holding on to his father. The two of them disappeared from the patio, leaving Cassie alone with Justin, who seemed content to stay in her arms. Compared to the sturdy Jason, Justin felt surprisingly light.

She sat down on one of the chairs at the poolside table and settled him on the glass top in front of her. Though taller and more dexterous than Jason, he hadn't started talking as well yet. Probably because he was too busy analyzing everything with that mathematical brain inherited from Ted.

Jason, on the other hand, never stopped making sounds and noises. He liked to hear his own voice and adored music of any kind, which was a good thing since Cassie played the piano and listened for hours to tapes of her favorite piano concertos while she designed and appliquéd her original quilts, pillows and stuffed animals.

"I know a silly song your grandma Arnold would sing to you if she were here." She kissed his pink cheek and took his hands, touching each finger as she sang. " 'Hinty, minty, cutie, corn, apple seed and apple thorn, Riar, briar, limber lock, six geese in a flock, Sit and sing, at the spring, o-u-t out again!' " She made his arms fly wide and he began to laugh, a real belly laugh that surprised and delighted her. They did this several times before Cassie heard a woman's call from another part of the house. Not long afterward, the trim sixtyish housekeeper appeared on the patio carrying two heaped plates of taco salad. Trace followed with the high chair in one arm and Jason in the other.

"I've got to meet the brave young woman who made it past Mrs. Blakesley and presented you with your son!"

She beamed at Cassie, who rose to her feet and balanced Justin against her hip while the older woman put the plates on the table. After wiping her fingers on her apron, she held out a hand, which Cassie shook. "I'm Nattie Parker and I have to tell you this is probably the most exciting day of my life! Talk about the spitting image!"

Cassie's eyes filled with tears as she looked at Jason. "He is, isn't he? And Justin is so much like my sister and her husband, I'm still in a daze. In fact, none of this seems real." She couldn't resist kissing Justin's silky blond head.

Nattie nodded in agreement. "That was a switch for the books. And to think you've been looking for Jason's daddy all this time, and Trace almost sent you away with the police. Shame on you, Trace," she said in a stern voice, but love for her employer shone through.

The woman's raisin-dark eyes fastened on Jason. "I can't wait another second to get my hands on him. He has the kind of solid little body you just want to squeeze, d'you know what I mean?"

"I know exactly," Cassie said, loving Nattie on the spot. She let her gaze wander to Trace, who was tenderly eyeing both his sons. One day Jason would grow into the same kind of vital, handsome, dynamic man....

At the moment, though, Jason was struggling with Nattie. He stopped when she handed him a cracker from her pocket; she gave another one to Justin with a quick kiss. "Come on, young man," she told Jason. "You can go with me to get the baby food. What would you like today? Beans and lamb? That's what your brother's having."

As she walked away chatting, Trace motioned Cassie to a chair. "Are you sure you want to feed Justin?"

"Positive," she asserted, placing him on her lap. Despite the cracker halfway in his mouth, he reached for the salad, which she pushed out of his way.

Turning her attention to Trace, who'd gone to the bar behind them, she said quietly, "Do you know what thrills me? He uses both hands in all his movements. That means he has the full use of his arm. He'll be able to do any sport or activity Jason can do." She paused to remove her fork from Justin's eager clutches. "Tell me what the doctors say about him."

Trace supplied napkins and iced fruit drinks before taking his seat. Their eyes met. "It's called an amniotic band. It tightened around his arm in the womb, cutting off some of the blood supply. The specialist says physical therapy to build up his muscles can begin when he turns three. By the time he's an adult, the defect will hardly be noticeable."

She leaned down and kissed Justin's smooth shoulder. "Well, aren't you the luckiest little boy in town. I wonder if you'll turn out to be as great a tennis player as your father. You're built just like him."

Trace looked pensive as he ate a forkful of salad. "Genes don't lie, do they?"

"No." She ate a mouthful of cheese and guacamole, then let Justin try a little of her pineapple drink.

"When did your sister first suspect Jason wasn't her son?"

"Her baby was rushed to the infant intensive-care unit as soon as he was born. A little later, the pediatrician told her he'd had trouble breathing on his own. She didn't actually hold him for about eight hours.

"When he was finally brought to her, his black hair and olive skin were so different from what she'd expected, she couldn't believe Jason was hers and told me as much over the phone. But since Susan's and my baby pictures show us with dark hair, I assumed Jason's hair would turn blond after a few months and didn't take her seriously. Until I saw him for the first time, that is."

Trace let out an audible sigh. "Unfortunately, I wasn't there for the delivery. The baby came sooner than we expected, and by the time I arrived at the hospital, Gloria was in her room and the baby was in the intensive-care unit. About a half hour later the pediatrician came to tell us about Justin. I went down to the nursery with the doctor and saw Justin for the first time lying in one of those cribs. The switch must have occurred in the unit."

She nodded. "Susan said the baby was born at 9:05 a.m."

Trace put down his fork and looked at her solemnly. "Our son was born at 9:04. And your sister was right. There were ambulances all over the place when I arrived. The chemical plant outside Phoenix blew up, killing a dozen people and sending dozens more to various hospitals. The place was swarming with hospital personnel, relatives, reporters. Because of all the confusion, I was delayed getting to Gloria's room."

She closed her eyes. "It sounds so impossible, so incredible, and yet that must explain why there was a mix-up. Do you think we should demand an investigation and lodge a formal complaint to prevent this from happening to anyone else?"

He was quiet so long she didn't know if he'd heard her. "Part of me says yes. Another part says accidents do happen, even when the greatest precautions are taken. Probably the chances of such a thing occurring again are something like a billion to one."

"I've thought that myself. We know it wasn't intentional."

After a pause he said, "In principle, I'm opposed to unnecessary litigation. This has become a sue-happy society. So, on balance, I'm against suing."

Cassie didn't realize she'd been holding her breath. "I'm glad you said that. I don't think I could handle an official investigation after everything I've been through in the last year with Ted's death—he was killed in an accident—and then Susan getting sick and...and dying." Not to mention Rolfe's recent engagement to a woman overseas, which had come as a painful shock to Cassie. She and Rolfe—her lifelong neighbor—had always been close, although she'd put off making a decision about marriage. But she'd assumed that when his studies were over, he would come home and they'd work things out.

"The newspapers would get hold of it and the publicity would be horrible," she said, shuddering at the prospect. "In the end, all it would do is damage the hospital's reputation and ruin people's lives. I don't want this to affect the boys."

"I agree," Trace concurred in a sober tone. "However, we will get those blood tests and I'm going to write the hospital board a letter informing them what happened. I'll let them know that, though we're not pressing charges, we are requesting an unofficial inquiry to satisfy our questions. Indirectly it might prevent another mistake like this in the future."

"I think that's best, and I know Susan and Ted would have felt the same way. Mr. Ramsey, did you or your wife ever have any suspicions that Justin wasn't your son?"

He cocked one dark eyebrow. "I think at this stage we should dispense with the formalities. My name is Trace, and the answer to your question is a definite no. Gloria is a tall willowy blond with hazel eyes. Everyone assumed Justin inherited her coloring and slender build. But after looking at your sister and brother-in-law's photograph, I can see the resemblance to Gloria is superficial at best. Justin bears an unmistakable likeness to both his parents."

Cassie nodded in agreement. She wanted to ask him more questions about his wife, but Nattie's entry with Jason and the baby food prevented her. Jason now sported a bib, which he was trying to pull off.

While Trace relieved her of his son and slipped him into the high chair, Nattie put the food on the table. "Here's a bib for my golden boy." She tied it around Justin's neck. "Now all of you have a good lunch. I'll hold any phone calls to give you a chance to talk."

Trace didn't let Nattie escape until he had pressed her hand in a gesture that spoke volumes about their relationship. Justin was surrounded by people who loved him, and that knowledge brought the first modicum of peace to Cassie's heart.

For the next while Cassie told Trace about Ted's fatal car accident en route to summer camp with the army reserve and Susan's subsequent depression, which led to one of her chronic bouts of pneumonia after a troubled pregnancy. Without Ted, she couldn't seem to endure.

Justin behaved perfectly while they talked. Half the time he managed the spoon by himself without making any mess. Cassie wished she could say the same for Jason. Though he loved the lamb, every time Trace gave him a spoonful of beans he'd keep them in his mouth for a minute, then let them fall back out. And worse, he smeared the top of his high chair so it resembled a finger painting.

Trace surprised her by being highly amused rather than irritated. She could hardly equate this patient caring man with the forbidding bank official who would have sent her from his office in handcuffs without a qualm.

Halfway through his peaches, Justin showed signs of being tired and his eyelids drooped. Jason was exhausted, as well. Unfortunately he tended to become even more restless and noisy before falling asleep.

She looked over at Trace who was chuckling at the funny sounds Jason made as he practically inhaled his fruit. "May I put Justin to bed?" she asked.

Trace flicked her a searching glance, then gently tousled Justin's hair. "Has too much excitement made my little guy sleepy? Why don't we take both of them upstairs? While you deal with Justin, I'll put Jason in the tub.''

Cassie tried to smother a smile but failed. ''I wish I could tell you Jason isn't usually this impossible at meals, but it wouldn't be the truth.''

His lips twitched. ''I'm afraid when my mother finds out about this, she'll tell you I was much worse. Like father, like son.''

Carefully lifting Justin, she rose to her feet. ''Does your mother live here in Phoenix?''

''Not only Mother but the entire Ramsey clan.''

''You're a large family, then?''

''I have two brothers and a sister, all of whom are older with children,'' he informed her as she followed him to a hallway on the other side of the patio.

By now Jason's bib had been removed and Trace held his food-smeared son firmly around the waist. ''Ma-ma, Ma-ma,'' Jason cried when he realized he was being swept away from their cozy domestic scene by this dynamic stranger.

''Da-da's got you, Tiger,'' Trace said, mimicking his son. Cassie's heart leapt in her chest. No man had ever had this physical effect on her, not even Rolfe. She'd loved him from childhood; he was the man she'd planned her future around. But the grief Cassie had suffered over her mother's death, followed by Ted's fatal accident and Susan's illness, had taken its toll. She wasn't ready to set a wedding date. Rolfe, hurt and disillusioned, had accused her of not being in love with him and had broken their engagement. The next thing she knew, he had gone abroad to study music.

He was a gifted musician who'd been offered more than one prestigious scholarship.

Before Susan died, she'd said that a separation was exactly what Cassie and Rolfe needed. They'd never spent more than a week or two away from each other, and a year's separation would clarify their feelings. When they came together again, there'd be no hesitation on either side if a marriage between the two of them was meant to be.

Susan's remarks made a lot of sense to Cassie. But she hadn't considered the possibility that Rolfe would fall in love with someone else in the interim, nor that it would hurt so much. Now Susan was gone and Cassie would never again be able to confide in the sister who'd always been her best friend and confidante.

"Cassie?" Trace called over his shoulder with a puzzled expression on his face. "Are you all right?"

"Yes. Of course." She smiled. "I had to stop for a minute and look at all these watercolors. They're fabulous, just like the ones in your office."

"My sister, Lena, is one of the most talented artists I know, but she's so critical of her own work, she refuses to display any of her paintings in public."

"So you do it for her," Cassie murmured. She couldn't help but be touched by his loyalty to his sister. It was ironic, and somehow pleasing, that while she'd been reliving bittersweet memories of her own sister, she'd been gazing at *his* sister's work—a sister he obviously adored. There were many surprising and wonderful facets to Trace Ramsey's personality, as she was beginning to learn. "How many of Lena's paintings have you sold?"

"None," he said as they reached the second floor. "She made me promise. In fact, she hasn't signed them. But if she ever changes her mind, my walls will be bare."

Cassie could believe it. In fact, there were several paintings here that gave her ideas for wall hangings and rugs, but they were fleeting images and she couldn't do anything about them now.

Justin's suite of rooms had the Southwest flavor of the rest of the house, but concessions had been made to practicality, creating a more traditional child's decor. Chocolate-brown shag carpeting covered the floors, and baby furniture filled the spacious room. A huge hand-painted mural took up one whole wall.

It was an enchanted-forest scene, with each little animal and insect possessing a distinct personality. Cassie was completely charmed by it and easily recognized the artist's hand. "Your sister painted this."

"Yes. That was Lena's gift to Justin," he called out from the bathroom. The minute the water started filling the tub, she could hear Jason's protests turn to squeals of delight. He always enjoyed his bath.

Cassie wondered if Justin liked the water, but she'd have to find out another time, because he was sound asleep, lying limp against her shoulder.

She gently placed him on his stomach in the crib and covered him with the cotton blanket. Automatically his thumb went to his mouth. He looked so blissfully content she didn't have the heart to pull it out again and risk waking him.

After leaning over to bestow one last kiss, she headed for the immaculate white bathroom accented, like the downstairs rooms, in natural wood. It was difficult to tell who was having a better time, Jason or his father.

Trace's white shirt-sleeves were rolled up above the elbows to display tanned forearms with a sprinkling of dark hair. His smile made him look years younger as he urged Jason to float on his back and kick his sturdy little legs. "That's it, Tiger. Make a big splash."

When water hit him in the face, he burst into deep-throated laughter. He sounded so happy that Cassie hated to disturb them. However, Jason had already caught sight of her standing there holding a fluffy tangerine-colored towel. He immediately tried to sit up, plaintively crying, "Ma-ma," and stretching out his arms.

"I'm afraid we've got to get going," she said apologetically to Trace who looked distinctly disappointed by the interruption. With undisguised reluctance, he wrapped Jason in the towel and started to dry him. "My luggage is being held at a motel in West Phoenix," Cassie went on. "We'll have to stop there on our way to the airport."

Trace frowned and she knew why. But he didn't understand what it was like to live on a budget. Even when her mother was alive and Susan was at home, they had all worked hard to make ends meet. And now that a future with Rolfe had slipped away, and with little Jason to support, she had to be more careful than ever how she spent her money.

In the short year and a half Susan and Ted had been married, they had acquired some insurance and savings. But before her sister's death, Cassie and Susan had agreed that any money would be invested for Jason's education. Cassie wouldn't have dreamed of touching it.

When she started to gather up Jason's soiled outfit, Trace told her to leave it for Nattie to wash. "He can wear something of his brother's for the flight back, can't you, Tiger?"

After diapering him on the bathroom counter, he reached into the drawer for a pale green stretchy suit with feet and put Jason into it. Then he playfully lowered his head to Jason's tummy and made a noise against it, producing a gale of infectious laughter from his dark-haired son.

In a very short time, Jason seemed to have overcome his fear of Trace. Much more of his father's attention and he wouldn't want to leave, a thought that troubled Cassie more than a little. This was his first experience with a man and he appeared to be enjoying it.

Cassie couldn't help wondering if her letter telling Rolfe about her plan to raise Jason as her own son had something to do with his recent engagement. His fiancée was another violinist, a woman he'd met in Brussels. Cassie was tempted to phone him long-distance, despite the cost; that way, they could really talk. Maybe expecting him to take on Jason if he married her was asking too much.

Then again, maybe he was truly in love with this other woman. Cassie was so confused she didn't know what to think. They'd been childhood sweethearts and had turned to each other whenever problems arose. She'd never stopped loving him and didn't think he'd stopped loving her, either.

Peeking in on Justin one more time, Cassie had to resist the impulse to kiss him, for fear of waking him. He looked like Susan while he slept, a fair-haired angel with flushed pink cheeks. Once again she felt that tug of emotion and hoped, somehow, that Justin's parents knew their little son was happy and well in Trace's home and heart.

In no time at all, Cassie had thanked Nattie and was following Trace outside to the BMW. Without giving her a choice, he ensconced her in the front seat. As he strapped his son in the back, she could tell he had some serious concern on his mind.

Once again he wore that look of determination. It made her uncomfortable, and she wished Jason was fussing so she'd have a reason to hold him in her arms as a buffer against Trace. But Jason's eyelids were fluttering, which meant he was ready to fall asleep any second.

When they had driven away from the house and were headed for the motel, Trace darted her a swift glance. "I want Jason close to me, Cassie," he said, using her name for the first time. "I've already missed his first nine months, and I refuse to lose out on any more time. I can tell you want to be with Justin just as badly. Let's be honest and admit the odd weekend here, the three-day holiday there, will never be enough for either of us."

Cassie had been thinking hard about that, too. Already the wrench of having to leave Justin hurt unbearably. But how soon would she be able to break away from her work to fly here again? With Christmas only three weeks away, this was her busiest time.

The money made from holiday sales would support her and Jason for at least five or six months. She didn't dare lose out on her most lucrative time of year. And her other job, playing piano for ballet classes four mornings a week, made it impossible to get away for more than a couple of days at a time.

"I agree with you, Trace, but I don't have any solutions, because I'm swamped with work and I know you are, too. I was going to suggest we trade the children from time to time."

The angry sound that came out of him made her shiver and immediately told her she'd said the wrong thing.

"Out of the question. As far as I'm concerned, six months with one parent, then six with the other is no alternative."

"I don't see that we have a choice."

"There's always a choice," he muttered in what she imagined was his banker's voice. "You could move to Phoenix with Jason."

She jerked her head around and stared at him in astonishment. "That would be impossible. I may not own a banking corporation, but my business is just as important to me. It relies on a clientele that's been built up over two generations of sewing for people. My mother taught Susan and me the business. Now I've branched into handicrafts. I wouldn't even know where to start if I had to relocate to a different city."

At this point they arrived at the motel. Without responding to her remarks, he got out of the car and went into the office to get her luggage. Within minutes he'd stashed it into the trunk and was back in the driver's seat. Before starting the car, he pulled a little black book from his pocket and asked for her address and phone number in San Francisco. Grudgingly she gave him the information; then they drove in painful silence to the airport, where he found a vacant space in the short-term parking lot.

He didn't immediately get out of the car. Instead he turned to her with a dangerous glint in his eye. "I'm warning you now that if we can't work this out, I'll take you to court and sue for custody of Jason."

"You don't mean that!" she burst out angrily, but the grim set of his jaw told her he did. Her heart was pounding so fiercely she was sure he could hear it.

"I'm his natural father and I'll be able to provide for his financial well-being in a way you never could. There isn't a judge in the state who would allow you to keep him. Bear in mind that the hospital will be called in to prove paternity and it could get messy."

"You told me you didn't approve of people who sued other people," she said, her voice shaking in fear and fury.

His eyes narrowed menacingly. "If you recall, I said, 'in principle.' But we're talking about Jason here, and what's best for him. You've already told me you're not married or even engaged." *But only because she'd put off Rolfe one too many times. Maybe it still wasn't too late.* "In fact," he continued, "I gathered from our conversation at lunch that you're not even dating anyone special who could help you raise him. You've only taken care of him for two months. You're not his parent. You're not even related."

"Now you listen to me!" Cassie whispered hoarsely, trying not to wake Jason by shouting. "I love that child with every fiber of my being. You're not related to Justin, either!"

"Justin's been my son since birth, and no judge will take him away from me. As his aunt, the most you can expect will be liberal visitation rights and a bill for exorbitant court costs and attorney's fees. Think about it, and give me your answer tomorrow night. I'll phone you at ten."

"Give you *what* answer?" she lashed out. "Do you know what you're asking? That I leave my whole life behind and move to a strange city with no friends, no support system, just so you can have your cake and eat it, too?"

"Naturally I'll provide for you and make sure you're comfortably settled until you can get your business going here. With my contacts, you would have no problem. Would that be such a penance when it means we would both have daily contact with the boys for the rest of our lives?"

Cassie didn't want to hear another word. "Aside from the fact that the idea is ludicrous, has it occurred to you what people would say? People who don't know the true situation? I noticed you didn't bother to explain anything to Mrs. Blakesley. She probably thinks I'm one of your mistresses who suddenly showed up to ask for money."

"I'm not particularly worried about what Mrs. Blakesley thinks," he countered smoothly.

"Maybe you're not concerned about your reputation, but I value my good name more than that!"

"More than you value a life with Jason and Justin?" His question was calculated to reduce her arguments to the trivial. But by now she was on to his tactics.

"You can phone me all day and all night, but it won't do you any good. I guess I'll have to take my chances and let the judge decide when I can spend time with Jason and my nephew. See you in court!"

She didn't, couldn't, hide the disgust and anger in her eyes or her voice. Jumping from the car, she yanked the back door and reached for Jason, who was still sleeping soundly. Trace finally got out of the car to collect her bags from the trunk.

Unable to bear his presence another second, she walked toward the terminal with the baby in one arm, her tote bag in the other. Right now she wanted to put as many miles as possible between them. All the way back to San Francisco, she regretted her trip to Phoenix and wished she'd never heard of Trace Ramsey.

CHAPTER THREE

CASSIE TAPPED on her neighbor's door and let herself in. "Beulah? I'm back."

After climbing all those steep streets from the ballet studio in the bitter cold, the apartment felt toasty and inviting. San Francisco had been locked in fog since the night she'd flown in from Phoenix more than a week ago. It seemed to penetrate everything, including the ski sweater she wore over her sweatshirt.

"I'm in the studio," Beulah Timpson called out. The older woman had been like a favorite aunt to Cassie and Susan, and had come close to being Cassie's mother-in-law. For as long as Cassie could remember, Beulah, a talented ceramist, had lived with her three children in the apartment above the Arnolds'.

Cassie and Susan had been best friends with Beulah's two daughters and her son, Rolfe. It was in her late teens that the close friendship Cassie shared with him gradually changed into something else. When Susan's and Cassie's mother fell ill with cancer, Rolfe became a source of strength. Cassie turned to him more and more, and learned she could always depend on him to offer help and compassion.

Soon after her mother's death, he told her he loved her and wanted to marry her. Cassie happily accepted his modest engagement ring; by that time they were both seniors at the university, studying music theory. He played the cello and she the piano.

Rolfe wanted to get married immediately after graduation, but Cassie couldn't see any reason for urgency, since they were constantly together, anyway, and had no money. She encouraged him to get his master's degree in music while she worked on expanding her home sewing business. A year down the road as a Ph.D student, he'd be able to earn extra money teaching undergraduates. By that time, she would have saved enough money for a small wedding and a honeymoon. They'd live in her apartment, since Susan had already married and moved to Arizona.

Unlike Susan, who married Ted within eight weeks of meeting him, Cassie wasn't in any hurry. She needed time to regain her emotional equilibrium first. The loss of their mother had been bad enough. But when she received the horrifying news of Ted's untimely death, Cassie went into a severe depression. At that point, her constant worry about her pregnant sister, whose history of chronic pneumonia put her at risk, made it impossible for Cassie to think about her own needs, or Rolfe's.

Then came a night when everything changed. For the first time since she'd known him, Rolfe didn't seem to understand. In fact, he refused to hear any more excuses and demanded that she set a wedding date—the sooner the better. Since they'd already been over that ground more than once, Cassie was surprised by his demands. She'd never seen him so insistent and unyielding. She asked him to leave the apartment, saying they'd talk again in the morning, when their nerves weren't so frayed.

But he stayed where he was. In a voice that shocked her with its anger, he accused her of using him. Cassie shook her head in denial, but he was obviously too hurt to listen to reason and asked for his ring back. When she begged him to be patient a little longer, the bitterness in his eyes revealed his hurt and disillusionment. He retorted that he hadn't pressured her to live with him because she didn't approve of premarital sex. And since she couldn't set a date for the wedding, he had to conclude she wasn't in love with him.

Cassie hadn't been prepared for that, nor for his declaration that he'd been offered a fellowship to study in Belgium and had decided to accept it. He held out his hand and Cassie wordlessly returned the ring.

He left at spring break, plunging her into a different kind of despair, one of profound loneliness. But by then Jason had been born and Susan was seriously ill. Looking back on that dreadful period, Cassie wondered how she'd survived at all. If Jason hadn't needed a mother's love and attention even before Susan died, Cassie might have died of grief herself. And still Rolfe stayed away.

Through it all, Beulah never pried or made judgments. As a result, the two of them were able to remain firm friends. Now that her children lived in other parts of the state, Beulah seemed to encourage Cassie's friendship, even volunteering to tend Jason in the mornings.

Walking through the apartment to the workroom, Cassie found the older woman at her potter's wheel. She stopped short when she didn't see the playpen. "Where's Jason?"

Beulah was throwing clay and didn't pause in her movements. "He's downstairs in your apartment with his daddy."

"Beulah! You didn't!"

"I did." She concentrated on her work for a moment. "First of all, he's not here to kidnap Jason. He assured me of that and I believe him." Her voice was calm and matter-of-fact. She glanced up at Cassie, smiling. "The two of them are carbon copies of each other, just like you said. Since Jason seemed perfectly happy to go with him, I couldn't see that it would hurt. I never saw a man so crazy about a child in my life. Watching them together made my Christmas."

All the while she was talking, Cassie held on to the nearest counter for support. *She should have known he would come.* Hanging up on him every time he called had probably infuriated him. But she had none of the answers he wanted to hear.

After agonizing over the situation for endless hours, Cassie had decided a judge would have to sort it out. Though she ached to know and love Justin, it was clear that her nephew's world was complete and revolved around Trace. If she was patient, the law would eventually dictate visitation rights so she could get close to Susan's son.

As for Jason, she'd hang on to him as long as possible. There was no doubt in her mind that she'd lose him in the custody battle Trace was planning. In fact, he'd probably come to San Francisco to make sure she'd given him the right address before he had her served with papers. His presence meant she couldn't prolong the inevitable confrontation.

"Well? Aren't you going to go find the man and say hello? He flew all the way from Phoenix early this morning to see you. What are you afraid of?"

"I'm going to lose Jason."

"Nonsense. From everything you've told me about him, he isn't the kind of man who'd cut you out of Jason's life. Especially once he knows the personal sacrifice you went through trying to find him in the first place. Cassandra Arnold, it's because of you that he's been united with a son he didn't know existed. Do you think he's going to forget a thing like that? Or the fact that Justin is Susan's child?"

"You weren't there when he threatened me with a custody suit." She shuddered at the memory.

"No, I wasn't. But that was a week ago, and he's had time to think since then. So have you. The least you can do is hear what he has to say. You owe him that much after refusing to take his phone calls."

Since there was no help from that quarter, the only thing left to do was go downstairs and see him, get it over with.

A feeling of dread formed a knot in her stomach as she thanked Beulah and headed for the ground-floor apartment, which was the only home she'd ever known.

After their mother's death, Cassie and Susan had taken over her business and pooled all their resources so they could continue to live there. When Susan and Ted moved to Arizona because of his job, Cassie stayed in the apartment. Although half the contents went off to Phoenix in the moving van, the place was still crowded to overflowing with furniture and mementos accrued over a lifetime. Cassie took the opportunity to clean house and quickly turned her home into a crafts shop of sorts. Right now, it was filled with Christmas orders—quilts, afghans, wall hangings, pillows, rag dolls, hand puppets, stuffed animals... The list went on and on.

Every nook and cranny of the small living and dining room contained evidence of her handiwork. Trace wouldn't be able to find a place to sit down. Even the top of the upright piano and bench were covered with stuffed Santas, reindeer and gingerbread men.

The two bedrooms were even worse. She kept her sewing machine and all the patterns and materials in her room, which hardly left enough space for her to crawl into bed at night.

Jason's room had become the depository for the larger stuffed animals and figures. They stood side by side, lined up against all four walls.

By Christmas Eve she should be able to find her furniture again. She'd had to put their two-foot Christmas tree with its homemade ornaments in the middle of the kitchen table. Jason loved the miniature lights and stared at them in fascination while he played with his food.

Taking a deep breath, Cassie entered the kitchen through the back door. She could hear Jason's shrieks of delight coming from the vicinity of his room. He was obviously thrilled to have his father there, and Cassie had to admit that fatherhood seemed to come naturally to Trace. It was possible that he'd already been given a court date; in that case, it wouldn't be long before Jason went to live with him and Justin.

She felt a pain in her heart as real as if she'd been jabbed with a knife. Maybe it was best he had come, after all. She couldn't live with the anxiety any longer.

Pushing the bedroom door open a little wider, she peeked inside. Jason was sitting in front of Trace, who was dressed in cords and a crew-neck black sweater, lying full-length on the carpet with his back toward her. His dark head rested on the five-foot-long green alligator Cassie had made for Susan. She'd added yellow yarn, to represent Susan's blond hair, and sewn the word "mommy" on the tail.

In Trace's hand was the eighteen-inch baby alligator with a green-and-yellow body and black yarn for hair; it bore Jason's name on the tail. He continued to tease Jason, tickling him gently and making him laugh so hard he was thrashing his arms and legs.

Suddenly Jason saw Cassie. He pointed a finger and tried to say, "Ma-ma," but couldn't get the words out and laugh at the same time. Alert to his every movement, Trace turned over on his back, resting his hand on the alligator's head.

His blue eyes searched hers for a long breathless moment. At least they didn't freeze her out as they'd done at the airport. "Hello, Cassie." Slowly his gaze traveled from her sweater-clad figure to her wind-blown hair and cheeks turned pink from the cold out-side. "Your neighbor let us in. She seemed to think it would be all right."

Strangely affected by the intimacy of his look, Cas-sie smoothed the curls from her forehead in a nervous gesture. "I'm sorry you couldn't find a place to sit."

A smile lurked at the corner of his mouth. "Since Justin came into my life, I've discovered the floor is a wonderful place to be. You meet all kinds of fascinat-ing creatures." He rubbed his thumb over the alliga-tor's glassy eyes. "Do you know I'm feeling deprived? There's no daddy alligator. I'm putting in an order for one right now. About six feet long with wild black hair and a scary grin, just like Jason's."

It sounded very much as if he was extending the ol-ive branch. How could he be talking this way when they had resolved nothing? She was still reeling from the bitterness of their last encounter.

"Come on, Jason. It's time for a nap." She stepped over Trace and scooped the baby up from the floor. Trace stayed where he was while she changed Jason's diaper and put him in his crib with a bottle. It was ac-tually time for his lunch, but she'd feed him later, af-ter his father had left.

Right now she needed to know what Trace had on his mind, and she didn't want Jason upset if the con-versation turned into another angry battle. "Let's go into the kitchen. Jason will settle down in a little while.''

By tacit agreement they left him crying. She knew he was wailing out his disappointment and fury; he'd been having such a wonderful time, and then she'd come along and spoiled everything. It didn't make Cassie feel any better. But this talk with Trace was crucial—and there was no sense in postponing it.

When they reached the kitchen, she offered him a seat and began to fix cocoa for both of them. Nobody was going to say she was uncivilized on the way to her execution!

Because of the fog, the room was darker than usual, and the lights on the tree twinkled all the more cheerfully. Suddenly she felt too warm, with Trace so close and vital and alive. She pulled off her ski sweater and hung it over a chair back.

When she'd prepared the hot chocolate, she placed their mugs on the table and sat down opposite him. Briskly pushing the sleeves of her navy sweatshirt up to the elbows, she began, ''I shouldn't have hung up on you—'' she paused for a deep breath ''—even though I was angrier than I've ever been in my life.''

''I wasn't exactly on my best behavior last week,'' he admitted gravely. ''Court isn't where I want to settle our problems.''

Cassie had been expecting to hear anything but that. ''I—I know how much you love Jason. He's your flesh and blood. The problem is I love him, too.'' Her voice had that awful quiver again. ''And I love Justin because he's part of my flesh and blood.''

"I know." He sounded totally sincere.

She raised tortured eyes to him. "No matter how I try to come up with a satisfying compromise, it sounds horrible becau—"

"Because that's precisely what it is. A compromise," he finished for her. "The only way I see out of our dilemma is to get married. That's why I'm here. To ask you to consider the idea seriously."

"Married?" She felt the blood drain from her face. In the interim that followed, Jason's cries sounded louder than ever.

Trace took a long swallow of cocoa. "Surely I don't have to point out the advantages to you. With everything legal, your reputation won't suffer, Justin and Jason will have a mother *and* a father, and we'll have the joy of raising the children together in our own home."

"But we don't love each other!"

He gazed steadily into her eyes. "Our marriage will be a business arrangement. Separate bedrooms. You'll be able to start up your crafts shop in Phoenix without the worry of having to meet the monthly bills. And I'll have the satisfaction of going to work every day knowing the boys are with the only person who could ever love them as much as I do."

Her hands tightened around the mug. "But you're still young, Trace. One day you'll meet someone you truly want to marry. Just because your first marriage didn't work out doesn't mean there isn't someone else in your future."

"That works both ways, Cassie," he said in a deceptively soft voice. "You're a very attractive woman. I'm surprised you didn't get married years ago." *Rolfe tried,* a niggling voice reminded Cassie. "But the fact remains, I've been married once in the full sense of the word and have no particular desire to repeat the experience. As far as I'm concerned, the only issue of importance here is the children. They need *us,* you and me. And they need us *now!* Some experts say that the first three years of a child's life form his character forever. If that's true, I would prefer if you and I were the ones guiding and shaping the boys' lives."

She couldn't sustain his penetrating glance and pushed herself away from the table. In two steps she'd reached the window, but even if the mist hadn't been so thick, she wouldn't have seen anything.

What Trace Ramsey had proposed was a marriage in name only. A marriage of convenience, her mother would have called it. Cassie had heard the term, but she'd never known anyone who had entered into such an arrangement. It sounded so cold-blooded. No expectations of physical or romantic love. Just a convenient solution to a problem that concerned them both. The children needed parents, and she and Trace Ramsey could honorably fill that need and still stay emotionally uninvolved.

She heard the scrape of Trace's chair against the linoleum as he stood up and came to stand next to her. "I know what you're thinking, Cassie. You're considerably younger than I am, and you have a right to a life of your own. But as long as we're discreet, we could see other people on the side, no questions asked. If some time down the road either of us wanted out of our contract to marry someone else, well . . . we'd face that when it happened.''

She gripped the edges of the sink so hard her knuckles turned white. "I think you're forgetting your ex-wife. Maybe she never bonded with Justin because, like Susan, she sensed he wasn't her baby. If she was to see Jason, isn't it possible she'd fall in love with him? I could certainly understand if she wanted another chance at marriage with you under those circumstances.''

Cassie wheeled around so she could read his honest reaction, but that was a mistake. Her kitchen was minuscule even with no one in it; now, with Trace blocking her path and the faint scent of his soap filling her nostrils, she felt almost claustrophobic.

"I'm way ahead of you, Cassie," he replied evenly, his hands on his hips. "I phoned her the evening you left Phoenix, but she was still in chambers so I sent her an overnight letter.''

"And?" She held her breath, unsure what she wanted Trace to tell her.

"She never responded.''

"Maybe she hasn't had time, or hasn't even seen the letter.''

"You're very generous to make excuses for her, but no." He shook his head. "I talked with Sabie, her housekeeper. Gloria read the letter.''

"And she didn't want to see Jason immediately?" Cassie cried, incredulous.

"I knew she wouldn't. But on the off chance that she'd gone through a complete character change, I told her to let me know and I would make it possible for her to spend time with Jason. Otherwise, if I didn't hear from her, I would assume it made no difference to her."

"But Jason is her own baby!"

Something flickered in his eyes. "Not all women have motherly feelings, Cassie. She never pretended to be anything but what she is, a remarkable attorney who is now a city-court judge and hopes to one day sit on the Supreme Court."

Cassie couldn't comprehend it. Talk about opposites attracting! She might search the earth and not come up with a more caring, devoted father than Trace. "Did you know she felt this way before you married her?" she asked in a quiet voice.

"If I hadn't made her pregnant, we would never have married."

She swallowed hard as she tried to take in what he was saying. "Didn't you love her?"

"We cared for each other. We also understood each other. Marriage was never in our plans, and I knew she'd give up the baby for adoption. I found I couldn't let her do that, so I struck a bargain with her. We would stay married long enough to satisfy protocol, then divorce with the understanding that I received custody of the child."

She blinked. "How often does she visit Justin?"

"She doesn't. She never has."

"Not once?" Her eyes grew huge.

He reached out and smoothed a stray curl from her forehead. At his touch her body trembled. The same gesture from Rolfe had never affected her this way. "That's why her lack of response to my letter doesn't surprise me. Is there anything else I can clear up for you?"

Needing to put distance between them, she slid past him and gathered the mugs from the table. "What would your family think?"

His wry smile seemed to mock her. "Whatever we want them to think. We can tell them that the moment we met, it was love at first sight. Or we can say nothing and let them draw their own conclusions. I'm a big boy now. I don't need my family's approval for what I do."

Her mouth had gone so dry she could hardly swallow. "I don't like lies."

"Then we'll tell them the truth. That we've decided to get married to provide a home for Justin and Jason. Period."

When he put it like that, so bluntly, she didn't know what to say. "E-Excuse me a minute, I have to check on the baby."

To her surprise he shifted his position, preventing her from leaving the kitchen. "I have a better idea. I'll leave—to give you time to think over my proposal. I'm at the Fairmont. Call me there when you've made your decision."

Her heart started to hammer. "How long will you be in San Francisco?"

"As long as it takes to get an answer from you."

She averted her eyes. "If the answer's no, what will you do?"

The muscles of his face went taut. "You're going to say yes. The boys need you too much. In your heart, you know it's the only solution. What was it your sister said before she died—*Find my son and take care of him for me?* Now you can honor her request and be Jason's mother at the same time."

On that note he disappeared from the kitchen and out the front door of the apartment.

So many thoughts and emotions converged at once that Cassie couldn't stand still. As if on automatic pilot, she tiptoed to Jason's room and discovered him sound asleep in a corner of his crib, with his cheek lying on his bottle.

The poor darling had finally worn himself out. Gently she pulled the bottle away and covered him with a light blanket. She thought of seeing him only on holidays, of missing his first steps and not being able to take him to kindergarten on his first day of school....

If she married Trace, she would have the luxury of being a mother to Justin, as well. The four of them would be a real family, in almost all the ways that mattered. Many things about Trace still remained a mystery, but the one thing she knew beyond any doubt was his devotion to the boys.

Not every man would have married his lover to obtain custody of his unborn child. And a small voice told her not every man would have wanted Jason on sight—no matter that Jason was the son of his body, no matter how precious he was. In that regard Trace Ramsey was a remarkable man.

Was it enough? Would it be enough for her? Could she marry him knowing the most important ingredient in the marriage was missing? Knowing that because of their loveless arrangement, she would never have a baby of her own?

Maybe Trace could conduct an affair on the side; in all probability he was seeing someone right now. But Cassie wasn't made that way and knew herself far too well. Perhaps her ideas were old-fashioned and out of date, but if she took marriage vows, she would hold them sacred until she died. Or until Trace asked her for a divorce....

Was that what worried her most? That one day he would fall deeply in love and want a real marriage with the woman who had captured his heart? The thought left Cassie feeling strangely out of sorts and depressed, which made no sense at all.

She'd wondered more and more about the things Rolfe had said to her the night he'd walked out. With hindsight, she could see how much she'd hurt him by putting him off. But during that long dark period, she hadn't been capable of making a decision, hadn't been ready to make a commitment. Instead of clinging to him as his wife, she'd left him hanging while she dealt with her grief.

And her refusal to go to bed with him had probably planted more seeds of doubt. But Cassie's mother had raised her girls to value their virginity, to reserve physical passion for their husbands. That was why

Susan was so eager to get married. In fact, Susan's intense feelings for Ted were so different from Cassie's easygoing, comfortable relationship with Rolfe they weren't even in the same league.

Susan and Ted couldn't stay away from each other, couldn't keep their hands off each other. Cassie had never been able to relate to those feelings. She loved Rolfe and always would, but she could wait until their honeymoon to express her love.

If she married Trace, there would be no problems in that area because he wouldn't be making physical demands on her. He'd be seeing other women. She was sure he'd be the soul of discretion. The little she knew about Trace told her he'd go to great lengths to keep his private life private, so no gossip could hurt the boys. They meant everything to him.

So why was she hesitating? Was she hoping against hope that Rolfe would break his engagement and come back to San Francisco to take up where they'd left off? How had Rolfe been able to fall in love with another woman so fast? Was it because his fiancée was willing to sleep with him? Cassie tried not to think about him sharing intimacies with anyone else, because it hurt. And, she supposed, because it was humiliating.

If they *were* sleeping together, that meant Rolfe wasn't really missing Cassie. And if that was true, then he'd gotten over the pain of Cassie's rejection and was making plans for a future that didn't include her. But it hadn't been a rejection, only a plea for more time.

So where did that leave Cassie? She had no guarantee that a man would ever come along to love her, body and soul. At least if she married Trace, she'd be able to indulge her longing to be a mother. Otherwise she would remain on the fringes of Jason and Justin's lives, never really involved. She couldn't bear that.

For the rest of the day she kept busy playing with Jason and putting the finishing touches on an order for a pear tree with partridges. After six o'clock, the doorbell rang continuously with customers placing and picking up orders.

Not until she'd tucked Jason into bed and cleaned the kitchen did Cassie work up enough nerve to reach for the phone. It was almost eleven and she'd run out of reasons not to call. She'd made her decision.

Her heart pounded in her ears as she asked to be put through to Trace Ramsey's room, but after ten rings and no answer she hung up. Maybe he was out, or had gone to bed. Whatever the case, she'd have to wait until morning.

Perhaps it was just as well. If she awakened tomorrow still feeling she was doing the right thing, then she'd try to call him again.

Feeling oddly deflated despite her tension, she unplugged the Christmas-tree lights and took a long hot shower. She checked on Jason one final time, then hurried into her own bedroom, eager for sleep. As she turned down the covers, she thought she heard a knock at the door.

Beulah was the only person who ever bothered her this late at night, and she always phoned first. Cassie had never had trouble before, but there could always be a first time. With the stealth of a cat she tiptoed to the living room and listened to see if she'd been mistaken.

After a minute she heard another rap. "Cassie?" a voice called out in hushed tones. "It's Trace. Are you still up? I didn't want to wake Jason if I could help it."

Trace?

A kind of sick excitement welled up inside her. She braced her hand against the door for support.

"Just a minute," she whispered and rushed to the bedroom for a robe. After opening the door she belatedly remembered that her hair was still damp from the shower. Her natural curls had tightened into a mop of ringlets that only a good brushing could tame.

He stared down at her, the hint of a smile lurking in his startling blue eyes. The moist night wind off the bay had tousled his hair, and he wore a fashionable bomber-style jacket made of a dark brown suede. Cassie had no idea he could look so... so...

"The answer's yes, isn't it?" he said matter-of-factly. "Otherwise you'd have called me hours ago and told me to go back to Phoenix and start court proceedings. Because one thing you're not, Cassie, is a coward."

CHAPTER FOUR

"Miss Arnold?" Nattie's voice carried to Justin's bedroom, which now contained a second bed for Jason.

Cassie turned as Trace's housekeeper entered the nursery. "Can't you and Mike bring yourselves to call me Cassie? I realize Trace only brought me and Jason to Phoenix twenty-four hours ago, but you and your husband have been so wonderful helping us to settle in, I feel like we're good friends already."

The older woman's eyes lit up. "If you're sure."

"I am. So, what is it?" She returned to the job of fastening an uncooperative Jason into his new outfit.

"Trace asked me to take over in here so you can finish getting dressed. He's one man who likes to be on time—particularly for his own wedding. I'll finish doing those buttons and take Jason downstairs to Justin and his daddy."

"I appreciate the offer, but he's dressed now," Cassie murmured as she slipped on his little white shoes and tied them with a double knot so he wouldn't kick them off. She gave him a kiss on the cheek and handed him to Nattie, who promptly carried him out of the room.

Cassie followed her more slowly and then headed to her own room. There were three guest bedrooms on the upstairs floor of the house, with the nursery at one end and Trace's private suite of rooms at the other. Since he'd told Cassie to choose a bedroom for herself, she'd picked the one closest to the children. That way she'd be able to hear them if they cried during the night.

Though the smallest of the three, her room had its own ensuite bathroom, and the wicker furniture plus the charming window seat created a cozy feeling that immediately made her feel at home. She'd already spent several hours gazing out over the fascinating desert landscape, with the mountains in the distance.

Off-white walls and soft yellow trim blended beautifully to give the room a timeless dreamy feeling. Large green plants stood grouped in one corner; they were reflected in the sheen of flawless hardwood floors stained a warm honey tone.

Cassie couldn't wait to design an area rug that would incorporate the room's colors in all their subtlety. But her thoughts were far removed from that particular project as she finished dressing for her wedding.

If the image in the mirror didn't lie, she *looked* like a bride. She wore the trappings of a bride—large, marquise-shaped emerald ring on the third finger of her left hand, matching emeralds on her ears, which were a wedding present from Trace, a cascade of orange blossoms on the shoulder of her simple white Thai silk dress with its scooped neck.

Five weeks ago she'd been living with Jason in San Francisco, heartbroken over her sister's death and Rolfe's engagement, working furiously at two jobs in order to build a business that kept her busy all hours of the day and night.

Right now, that Cassie seemed a different person. Trace had pampered her so thoroughly she hardly recognized herself anymore. Once she'd agreed to marry him, he had taken time off from his banking affairs to stay in San Francisco both before and after Christmas. He'd helped her with Jason and made all the preparations for the marriage and her move to Phoenix. Meanwhile she'd wound up her business and called her old friends with the news—friends she'd hardly seen in the past three years. Her responsibilities had made a social life impossible.

Not since Rolfe's tenderness at the time of her mother's death had she experienced anything approaching this extraordinary feeling of being looked after, taken care of. In fact, Beulah—who to Cassie's surprise approved of their forthcoming marriage—commented that all Cassie had to do was mention something and Trace had it done before she turned around.

When Cassie asked if they could be married before she met his family, with only the babies and Nattie and Mike for witnesses, Trace agreed to her wishes and arranged a private ceremony at the county clerk's office.

In certain ways, Trace was the equivalent of a fairy godfather, and even if their marriage wasn't a normal one, she knew she was a very lucky woman. She told herself not to dwell on the past or reminisce about what might have been. But it was impossible to forget that for most of her life she had imagined walking down the aisle with Rolfe.

Without conscious thought she pulled his framed picture from a box of mementos she hadn't yet put away. She sank down on the bed to study his lean, ascetic face one more time. She couldn't help wondering what he'd thought when he received her letter. She'd informed Rolfe that she was planning to be married after Christmas. She'd told him the truth—that she'd accepted Trace's proposal in order to be a legitimate mother to both boys. She also admitted that she still loved him, that she would always love him and hoped he'd forgive her for ever hurting him.

When there was no return letter from Belgium, Cassie had to accept the fact that he was truly lost to her, but it still hurt. "Oh, Rolfe . . ." She wept quietly for the many memories and the dream that was gone.

"*Cassie?* Are you ready yet?"

At the sound of footsteps she panicked and thrust the picture beneath one of the pillows on her bed. But she was too late. Trace had seen the betraying gesture and in a few swift strides crossed the room and reached for the frame.

After studying the photo for several seconds, he raised his head and stared at the moisture beading her eyelashes. "I've seen this man's picture before. In Beulah Timpson's place."

His face hardened and a dull red tinged his smooth-shaven cheek and jaw. She was immediately reminded of the implacable man she'd originally met, the one who had accused her of being part of a kidnapping scheme. "What's going on, Cassie? When I brought you here to see Justin that first day, you told me you were unattached. I assumed you were telling the truth." His voice barely concealed his anger.

Cassie slid off the bed, furious with herself for having inadvertently caused this friction when he'd gone out of his way to make everything so wonderful. From the beginning Trace had been completely honest with her; he deserved the same consideration.

"I grew up with Rolfe," she began in a low voice. "We were once engaged, but things didn't work out. He asked for his ring back, and now he's engaged to someone else, someone he met in Europe. I was saying goodbye to past memories. That's all." She gazed straight at him as she spoke.

Trace searched her eyes, as if looking for some little piece of truth she might have withheld. "The ceremony takes place at eleven. We still have forty-five minutes. It's not too late to back out."

"No!" she cried instantly, surprising even herself with her vehemence.

He pondered her outburst for an uncomfortably long moment. "Be very sure, Cassie—and not just for the boys' sake."

For some reason his comment sent her pulses racing. "I am," she answered without hesitation, realizing she meant it.

He squared his shoulders and the tautness of his facial muscles seemed to relax. He tossed the picture onto a stack of photos piled in a cardboard box beside her bed. "Let's go, shall we?"

The next hour flew by as Mike took pictures of Cassie and Trace holding the children, both before and after they arrived at the courthouse. Justin fussed because he'd come down with a cold. When the justice of the peace appeared and announced that it was time, Justin didn't want to let go of Trace, and that started Jason crying, too. Poor Nattie and Mike had to hold the children and try to pacify them while Trace grasped Cassie's hand and led her to the center of the room.

Despite the noise and impersonal surroundings, Cassie felt the solemnity of the occasion and wished more than ever that her mother and Susan were alive to share this moment with her. They would have loved Trace on sight. Not even Beulah was immune.

Out of the corner of her eye she darted a glance at her husband-to-be, who stood erect and confident. His snowy white shirt and midnight-blue suit not only enhanced his attractiveness but underlined his power; the red carnation he wore in his lapel added a note of festivity and joy. *I'm actually marrying this man,* she mused in awe and felt her heart turn over.

The justice of the peace bestowed a warm smile on them. "Cassandra Arnold and Trace Ellingsworth Ramsey, after this ceremony, today will be the first day of your life as a married couple. You've come together in the sight of God and these witnesses to

pledge your troth. Do you know what that means?"
He eyed them soberly, capturing Cassie's whole attention.

"It means commitment and sacrifice. It means enduring to the end, long after the fires of passion are tempered with the earning of your daily bread. It means forgetting self and living to make the other person happy, no matter the season or circumstances. Will you do that, Cassandra? In front of these two witnesses, do you take this man, of your own free will, to be your lawfully wedded husband?"

Cassie felt Trace's heavy-lidded gaze upon her. "Yes."

"And you, Trace? Of your own free will and in front of these two witnesses, are you willing to take Cassandra to be your lawfully wedded wife, to assume this solemn responsibility of caring for her all the days of your life? Are you willing to put her before all others, emotionally, mentally and physically?"

Cassie thought his hand tightened around hers. "Yes," came the grave reply.

"If you have rings to exchange, now is the time. You first, Cassandra."

Cassie had been wearing the simple gold band she'd bought for Trace on her middle finger so she wouldn't lose it. She quickly removed it and slid it on Trace's ring finger. The fit was perfect, and he gave her a private smile that unaccountably stirred her senses.

"Now you, Trace."

Cassie held out her left hand so Trace could nestle the white-gold wedding band next to the beautiful emerald engagement ring he'd given her on the plane as they'd flown to Phoenix. His movements were sure and steady.

"That's fine." The officiant smiled once more. "Now, by the power invested in me by the state of Arizona, I pronounce you husband and wife. It's not part of the official ceremony to kiss the bride, but..."

Before the man had even finished speaking, Trace's head descended and his mouth swiftly covered Cassie's as he pulled her close, sending a voluptuous warmth through her body. Cassie hadn't expected more than a chaste kiss on the lips. She wasn't prepared for the heady sensation that left her clinging to the lapels of his suit.

"Ma-Ma! Ma-ma!" Jason's and Justin's cries slowly penetrated her consciousness. Cassie moaned in shock and embarrassment, and broke the kiss Trace seemed reluctant to end. In that split second before she turned her burning face away, she thought she saw a smoldering look in his eyes. But by the time he lifted his head, it was gone. She decided she'd imagined it.

Moving out of her husband's arms, she shook the officiant's outstretched hand and thanked him, then hurried over to Nattie. Still holding Jason, the older woman gave her an awkward hug and murmured her congratulations. She handed the uncontrollable child to Cassie with a wry smile of relief.

He calmed down at once and started pulling orange blossoms out of her corsage. Trace was equally busy trying to pacify Justin, while Mike continued to take pictures. Cassie took one look at the flush on Justin's

fair skin and said, "Trace, I think we'd better leave for
the hotel. Justin should be in bed. He needs something to bring down his fever."

Within a few minutes the children were strapped
into their seats in the back of Trace's sedan. Cassie
hugged Mike and Nattie and thanked them again for
everything, then at Trace's urging got into the car and
they drove off.

The resort hotel, a few miles away in Scottsdale, had
sent a basket of fruit and a congratulatory bottle of
champagne to their suite. There were also two cribs;
amused, Cassie wondered what the management
thought about that as she busied herself putting the
boys to bed, while Trace dealt with all the baby bags
and luggage.

The hotel offered baby-sitting services, but Cassie
didn't feel comfortable about leaving Jason and Justin with a stranger just yet. She urged Trace to go for
a swim in the pool and relax. But he insisted on staying to help her settle the children, after he'd ordered
lunch to be served in the room where he'd put his bags.

By the time both boys had fallen into an uneasy—
and, as it turned out, short-lived—sleep, their lunch
was more or less ruined. The pasta with its cream
sauce had grown cold, the salad was soggy, the chilled
white wine room-temperature. Cassie was too tired
and anxious to care. All her attention was focused not
on her new husband but on the two miserable little
boys. Trace seemed equally distracted.

What should have been a fun three-day holiday, a
chance for the four of them to really get to know each

other, lasted exactly one sleepless night. Justin couldn't keep anything in his stomach; he was content only when Cassie or Trace held him. And as soon as Jason saw that Cassie's attention was diverted from him, he wailed loudly, and not even Trace could settle him down for long.

At eight the next morning, they packed up the car and drove home, frustrated and completely exhausted. It had become apparent that they would have to take Justin to his pediatrician as soon as they got home; in fact, Trace had called ahead from the hotel. Leaving Jason with Nattie, the three of them went to the clinic. Cassie was anxious to meet the man who'd been taking care of Justin, because he would automatically become Jason's doctor, as well.

Although Justin didn't have anything seriously wrong, several days went by before he was restored to his normal sweet disposition. Several weary, emotionally draining days, especially for Cassie. She'd spent all her time with the children since Trace had returned to his office to deal with some very delicate negotiations in his planned buy-out of a small Southwest banking chain.

Then, on Friday morning Trace shocked her by announcing that he'd invited everyone in his family to an informal garden party that evening to meet his new wife and son. Understandably enough, they were consumed with curiosity about his unexpected marriage. Gathering all the relatives under one roof, he told Cassie, would provide the perfect opportunity to reveal the switch and to explain their subsequent decision to marry for the boys' sake.

Intellectually, Cassie saw the wisdom in getting it over with as soon as possible. Emotionally, she was numb.

Alone with Trace and the boys, she could relax as she performed the normal duties of a busy mother without worrying about others' reactions to their platonic union. Tonight, however, she would be on trial in front of a roomful of Trace's relatives—people who would draw their own conclusions about her motives for marrying a man who wasn't in love with her.

She couldn't blame them if they believed her to be a mercenary person attracted to his money and social prominence, someone willing to be bought in exchange for mothering his sons.

None of them would understand her bond with Jason or the happiness it brought her to raise him as her own son. Only Trace knew.

Cassie dressed in the same outfit she'd worn to her wedding and put on a fresh spray of orange blossoms Trace had thoughtfully sent her. Needing her husband's support as never before, she took a deep calming breath as she prepared to meet his family. She clutched Jason in her arms, hugging him tight, then mustered her courage and walked slowly downstairs.

From the landing she searched for Trace's dark hair among the group assembled on the patio. But she soon realized black hair dominated the family scene; there was only a sprinkling of sandy-brown and russet hair. She gazed down at the group, panicking just a little as she realized that the adults and children chatting with one another numbered at least forty.

Justin sat contentedly on his grandmother's lap, examining her pearl necklace—real pearls, Cassie was sure. His hair gleamed a pale gold in contrast to her coal-black tresses, swept back in an elegant chignon. His complexion was pale against her darker skin. Somewhere in her ancestry there must have been Indian blood. Even at seventy, Trace's mother was the most beautiful woman Cassie had ever seen. In fact, the whole family had more than its fair share of tall, good-looking people.

There was a sudden hush as Cassie walked out on the patio. Rolfe had often called her his "pocket Venus." And right now she was more aware than ever of her full curves and diminutive height. She felt even more conspicuous being the only person, aside from Justin, with a head of golden blond curls.

To her relief, Trace broke off his conversation with a man she guessed to be one of his brothers and strode toward her. In a light tan suit with an off-white Italian silk shirt open at the neck, he looked so incredibly handsome Cassie purposely glanced elsewhere to prevent herself from staring.

She thought he would reach for Jason. Instead, he slid a possessive arm around her waist and held her tightly against him. In confusion she gazed up at him, only to discover his eyes wandering over her face with unmistakable admiration.

At breakfast he had told her she would have nothing to worry about at the party. All she had to do was behave naturally and follow his lead. The trouble was, his act was too convincing, and she was distressed to find herself wondering how it would feel to be truly loved by this man. This complex man who presented a formidable, dynamic front to the public, yet could reduce her to tears with his sweetness when he kissed his sons good-night.

He turned to his family. "I know it came as a shock to hear that Cassie and I were married over the weekend. But what was I to do? My charming bride burst into my office a couple of months ago with an astonishing story—that Justin was really her nephew and that this little tiger was my natural son."

He reached for Jason, who'd been trying to wriggle out of Cassie's arms to get to his father. "It seems the babies were switched at birth." He paused dramatically at the incredulous murmurs around him. "We have subsequently found out that because of a disaster that stretched hospital resources to the limit, the infant intensive-care unit ran out of wrist tape. One of the nurses sent an orderly for more. When he returned, the identification bracelets were inadvertently put on the wrong babies."

The family's stunned reaction proved to be even greater than Cassie had imagined. For five minutes pandemonium reigned. It took another five before everybody settled down enough so that Trace could continue with the details. He briefly described the background—Ted's accidental death and Susan's unsuccessful struggle to throw off pneumonia, Susan's belief that Jason wasn't her son and Cassie's taking on the responsibility not only of raising her nephew but of uncovering the truth.

He kissed the top of Jason's curly head and unexpectedly smoothed a wayward lock of hair from Cassie's brow. Then, with a smile lighting his eyes, he said, "To make a long story short, the four of us got along so famously, we didn't want the fun to stop. So we decided to become a family." The sudden tremor in his voice added the perfect touch, almost convincing Cassie it wasn't an act. "Cassie, please meet my mother, Olivia Ramsey."

He turned to face the older woman. "Mother, may I present my wife, Cassandra Arnold Ramsey, and my son, Jason?"

"Trace!" Her cry held the joy Cassie had hoped to hear, dispelling her anxiety that Trace's mother wouldn't accept her new grandson—or her daughter-in-law.

While one of the wives relieved the older woman of Justin, Trace helped her to her feet. Dressed in deep-rose silk, she walked toward Cassie with the dignity of a queen.

"Welcome to the family, darling." She embraced Cassie warmly, then stood back, holding her lightly by the upper arms. Her deep-set, clear gray eyes searched Cassie's as if she were gazing into her very soul.

"I can't tell you how happy, how thrilled, I am by this news. Trace is my baby and he's always been my greatest worry. To see him settled at last, with a beautiful wife and two lovely children, has given me a whole new lease on life."

"Thank you, Mrs. Ramsey." Cassie could hardly form the words after the older woman's loving reception. That Trace's mother adored her youngest son was obvious. Cassie felt a sudden surge of guilt; she hated deceiving anyone, particularly this welcoming and truly gracious woman.

"Cassie, please feel free to call me Olivia, like my other daughters-in-law. 'Mrs. Ramsey' is so formal, isn't it?"

Cassie nodded, not trusting herself to speak as she blinked back tears.

"Mother?" Trace gently interrupted. "How about saying hello to my son. Jason?" He turned the baby around. "This is Nana. Na-na."

"Oh, Trace!" she cried, reaching for Jason, who showed all the signs of bursting into tears at the sight of so many strangers. "I can't believe I'm not thirty-three years old and holding you in my arms again. He's identical to you. Look, everybody! Another heartbreaker!"

Heartbreaker is right, Cassie thought, allowing herself a covert glance at her husband. He had probably been attracting the attention of the opposite sex since he'd been old enough to crawl!

But before she could dwell on that curiously disheartening fact, she and the baby were suddenly besieged with hugs and kisses. Such spontaneous warmth and affection made Cassie feel worse than ever about the pretense. All the cheerful joking from James and Norman, who'd introduced themselves as Trace's brothers, told her the family assumed Trace was in love. And everything he said and did tended to verify their assumptions.

But the excitement proved to be too much for the babies. Once Jason started crying, Justin quickly followed suit. Cassie extricated herself from a group of nieces who were fighting over who got to hold Jason and hurried to retrieve Justin, who was clearly unhappy being tended by one of his aunts.

The second he saw Cassie his tears stopped and a smile appeared. It was clear that during his brief illness, a bonding had taken place between them. He reached eagerly for her and wrapped his arms around her neck. Together they wandered over to the banquet table the caterers had laden with everything from luscious fresh pineapple slices to salads and salvers of prime rib. Catering staff brought flutes of champagne and glasses of sparkling juice for the children.

As she handed Justin a piece of banana, Cassie caught sight of a group of latecomers walking out on the patio. She saw Trace, still carrying Jason, break away from the others and move toward a slender, auburn-haired woman.

Lena. Cassie could tell by the tender expression on her husband's face that he had a soft spot for his only sister. From what he had told Cassie, Lena resembled their father, Grant Ramsey, who had died of a stroke a few years earlier, leaving his children to carry on and expand the family business.

From the distance, Cassie watched in fascination as Trace bent his head and filled Lena in on the details. Eventually Lena held out her arms to Jason, who refused to go anywhere and clung to his father. While everyone chuckled, Trace looked around until he spotted Cassie with Justin, then pointed her out to his sister. Lena left the group and hurried toward them.

Her hair had been drawn into a braid and hung over one shoulder. In comparison to Cassie's curves, Lena's build was thin and wiry. Except for the same proud chin, Cassie saw very little of Trace in his sister, whose pert nose and dark gray eyes made her face gamin rather than beautiful.

She leaned over to give Justin a kiss on the cheek, but he began to cry and tightened his hold on Cassie. Lena shrugged good-naturedly, then turned her attention to Cassie, eyeing her the way she might size up a scene she wanted to paint. "I'm Lena Haroldson, Trace's sister, and I have to tell you I'm speechless at the news. You have to be the reason Trace looks ten years younger tonight. If you can keep him this happy, I'll love you forever." She smiled warmly, then added, "Welcome to the family, Cassie."

Though the words were meant to be complimentary, Cassie's heart plummeted to her feet. It was obvious that Lena adored Trace and guarded his happiness jealously. And it was equally obvious that she was the one Ramsey Cassie would never be able to fool.

"Thank you, Lena. I—I'm going to try to make our home a happy one." At least that was the truth.

A mischievous smile lifted the corner of Lena's mouth. "I'd say uniting Trace with Jason is a giant step in the right direction. I want to hear all about it from start to finish, but tonight's not the right time. I suspect Justin needs to go to bed. How about lunch next week when you're settled in? I'll take you to my favorite restaurant."

"I'd love it." Lena would never know how much her friendliness meant to Cassie. "In fact, I've wanted to meet you ever since I first saw your watercolors in Trace's office. They're good—very good."

Lena shook her head, but by the way her eyes lighted up, Cassie could tell she was pleased. "Trace told you to say that, didn't he?"

"No," Cassie declared baldly. "He was too busy trying to haul me off to jail on a kidnapping-extortion charge."

"What?" Lena gasped. "That doesn't sound like Trace. I know he's got a tough reputation when it comes to business, but he wouldn't dare do such a thing to you!"

"I'm afraid I would and almost did," a deep voice interjected. "But in the nick of time this little fellow saved his mother from the long arm of the law, didn't you, Tiger?"

Surprised, both women turned to Trace who had approached them unnoticed. Apparently Jason had had enough partying for one night. His pale blue outfit was crumpled and stained with what looked like fresh strawberry. In spite of Cassie's precautions in double-tying his shoes, he had managed to kick one off, which Trace held in his free hand.

"Mama!" Always vigorous, Jason practically propelled himself out of his father's arms to reach Cassie. If it hadn't been for Trace's lightning reflexes, he would have landed on the floor. By now, Justin was being just as impossible and refused to allow Trace to hold him.

"Well, well, little brother." Lena grinned at Trace. "It looks like you've got competition."

Trace sent Cassie an enigmatic look that for some reason gave her an uneasy feeling. "I don't mind, Lena," he muttered. "Now if you'll excuse us, we'll put the children to bed. Be a sweetheart and hold down the fort till we come back." He bussed his sister's cheek, then slid one arm along Cassie's shoulders.

As they made their way inside, everyone crowded around to say good-night to the boys. Cassie smiled and laughed, though it all felt a bit forced. Trace was making her unaccountably nervous.

"You didn't have to help me," Cassie murmured as they entered the nursery together. "Please feel free to go downstairs. It isn't very nice for both of us to disappear."

"You sound like you're trying to get rid of me," he said softly, but there was no amusement in his tone. "If I leave you on your own, you'll probably stay up here the rest of the night."

Perhaps he hadn't meant to sound critical, but his remark stung, increasing the tension she could feel building between them. She put a fresh diaper on Justin and eased him into his sleeper while Trace did the same for Jason. "Your family's wonderful. I wouldn't dream of offending them."

"Be that as it may, you seem to have no qualms about offending me." He paused, not looking at her. "Do me a favor. When we go back downstairs, pretend to like me a little bit."

His words produced a wave of heat that scorched her neck and cheeks. "I—I had no idea I had done anything else. I'm sorry, Trace."

After a slight pause he said, "It's not conscious on your part. You always treat me as if I wasn't there. I've never felt invisible before and don't particularly like the sensation. I thought we could at least be friends."

"We are." Her voice quailed despite herself.

"You have an odd way of showing it. Friends normally look at each other and smile once in a while, enjoy a private joke. You, on the other hand, reserve your affection strictly for the children. But you can't use them as a shield all the time."

She wheeled around, baffled by the total change in him. "A shield?" she cried, forgetting for the moment that their voices would keep the babies awake.

The dangerous glint in his eye unnerved her. "I don't know what else you'd call it. There aren't very many newlyweds who'd take two babies on their honeymoon."

Honeymoon? Cassie was aghast and looked away quickly. "After the chaos of Christmas and the move from San Francisco, I thought we agreed a little vacation with the children was exactly what we needed...so all of us could get acquainted away from the pressures of work and other people."

"If you recall, you were the one who suggested the idea. I simply went along with it, because I assumed you'd allow the hotel baby-sitters to take over once in a while to give us some time alone."

"I was afraid to trust them, particularly when Justin was running a temperature."

His jaw hardened. "That particular hotel has an impeccable reputation, with licensed sitters, a full-time registered nurse and a doctor always on call. If Justin had shown the slightest sign of any complication, we would have had the best care available at a moment's notice."

Her hands tightened on the bars of the crib. "I had no idea you weren't agreeable to the idea. You should have told me."

"I did, repeatedly, but you chose to ignore my hints and continued to cling to the children. Justin has become impossible. He knows all he has to do is look at you and you're right there to cater to his every whim. There *is* such a thing as a surfeit of attention."

Had she been spoiling Justin? Was Trace afraid she'd supplanted *him* in Justin's affections?

"I—I'm sure you're right. I've probably gone overboard in an effort to make up for lost time."

Her words didn't seem to mollify him. "You may not be sleeping in my bed, but in all other ways you're my wife, and there are things I expect of you besides being a mother to the boys."

What things? She had no idea all this had been seething inside him. "I'm not sure I understand you."

"How could you? We haven't had a moment to ourselves since we met!" He paused. "As chairman of the board, I attend a variety of social functions, and I do a certain amount of entertaining myself. Now that I'm married, it would create unnecessary and possibly damaging speculation if you didn't accompany me and fulfill your role as hostess when we're dining at home with friends and business acquaintances. Naturally the children won't be invited to those events," he added sarcastically. "Did you think you were being hired as a nanny when you accepted my proposal?"

"Not in so many words," she admitted, so confused by his anger that she didn't know what to believe. "But when you came to San Francisco, I was caught up in my feelings and concerns for the children—to the point that I wasn't capable of looking beyond their needs."

"That was almost two months ago, Cassie. It's time we talked about *our* needs."

His remarks caught her completely off guard. "Trace," she whispered, "your family is waiting for us. I don't think this is the time for the kind of discussion you seem to have in mind." She rubbed her palms agitatedly against her hips, noting that his eyes followed her movements with disturbing intensity.

There was a beat of silence, then, "For once you're right." He kept his voice low. "But be aware that I intend to pursue this after we say good-night to the family. In the meantime I would appreciate it if you'd join me in creating a united front. Mother would never admit it to you, but she's not as well as she pretends."

Unconsciously Cassie's hand went to her throat. "What's wrong with her?"

"She had a heart attack recently. The doctors have warned her to slow down and take life easier. Since our marriage seems to have brought her so much pleasure, the last thing I want to do is upset her. She happens to believe that the greatest happiness in life is achieved through a good marriage. My divorce, I'm sorry to say, hurt her deeply, and ever since the attack she's been worried she might die before she sees me settled with a wife and family of my own."

Inexplicably Cassie felt a strange, searing pain. Was *that* his underlying motive for asking her to marry him? The marriage would guarantee his mother's peace of mind and explain her reaction when they were introduced earlier in the evening. It was yet another example of Trace's unswerving devotion and loyalty to those he loved.

She took a deep, shuddering breath. "You know I wouldn't deliberately do anything to hurt her."

His hands curled into fists, then relaxed, as if he had come to the end of his patience. "All I'm asking is that you try to act more natural and comfortable with me—even when the children aren't around." He sighed. "I don't understand you, Cassie. I can't figure out if you're still in love with your ex-fiancé, or if he did something to put you off men for good."

CHAPTER FIVE

TRACE GAVE HER no chance to respond. He grasped her hand and started for the hallway; she didn't try to resist. It shouldn't have come as any surprise that while they mingled with the family for the rest of the evening, he kept his arm firmly around her shoulders. It was a deceptively casual gesture, but Cassie knew that if she tried to pull away, she'd feel the bite of his fingers against her skin.

Shortly before the end of the party, as people were preparing to leave, he lowered his head to Cassie's ear. She couldn't tell if the caress of his mouth against her hot cheek was intentional or not, but his touch shot through her body like a spurt of adrenaline. "It's exceptionally warm tonight," he whispered. "Join me for a swim after everyone leaves... and we'll continue what we started upstairs."

She bit the soft underside of her lip. The thought of being alone with Trace in the swimming pool made her panic. Since the kiss he'd given her at their wedding, she'd become physically, sensually, aware of him—something that had never happened with Rolfe in all the years they'd spent together.

She found herself remembering things Susan used to say about Ted. "I never want to say good-night to him, Cassie. One kiss isn't enough. All he has to do is touch me and I go up in smoke. Everything about him fascinates me, even the way he chews his toast. If we don't get married soon, I don't think either of us can hold out any longer."

Frightened that he could feel her trembling, Cassie eased herself away from Trace's hold. "First I'll have to help Nattie clean up."

"Nattie's job is to supervise the caterers, who were hired for that express purpose, and Mike has a whole retinue of gardeners to put the grounds in order. In case you're about to offer any other excuses, you can forget them. Tonight I need to be with my wife. Is a midnight swim and a little honest conversation too much to ask?"

His question whirled around in her brain as she said good-night to Trace's family and escaped to her bedroom. Out of breath from an attack of nerves and a heart that was pounding out of rhythm, she leaned against the closed door. That was when she spied a gaily wrapped package sitting in the middle of her bed.

There had been so many gifts since her arrival in Phoenix, she certainly hadn't expected any more. Curious, she walked over to pick it up, wondering if someone in the family—Lena?—had thought to welcome her with something a little more personal. Quickly she unwrapped the box and lifted the lid. A handwritten card had been placed on the layers of tissue.

"It occurred to me," the card read, "that Justin's cold wasn't the only reason you wouldn't swim with me in Scottsdale. In case you didn't have a decent suit and hadn't found the time to shop for one, I took the liberty of picking something out for you. The green matches your eyes. I couldn't resist. Trace."

Carefully she moved aside the tissue paper and eased out a two-piece swimsuit. It was more modest than some of the bikinis she'd seen on the beach, but the fact remained that she'd never worn a two-piece before. Though slender, Cassie took after her mother in the full-bodied-figure department.

She'd always felt more comfortable in a one-piece outfit, but she wouldn't have been caught dead in the only suit she owned. It was so old and faded that she was planning to throw it out. Trace had probably guessed as much.

She flushed at the thought. It seemed he knew her better than she knew herself and refused to take the chance that she would use the lack of a proper swimsuit as an excuse for not meeting him at the pool.

Suddenly there was a rap on the door. "Cassie? I'm giving you five minutes. If you're not downstairs by then, I'll be back up to get you, and a locked door won't stop me. It would be a shame to ruin that lovely dress you're wearing, but I won't hesitate to throw you in, emeralds and all."

His threat galvanized her into action. In three minutes, her clothes lay everywhere and she'd put on her new swimsuit. She ran for her terry-cloth bathrobe, then dashed barefoot down the stairs.

BOTH OF THEM 93

The caterers must have cleared the tables in record time. When Cassie arrived on the patio, everything was quiet and only the lights from the swimming pool had been left on. The warm night air, sweet with the scent of sage blowing off the desert floor, felt like velvet against her heated skin. She'd never seen a more romantic setting in her life.

When she and Susan were little girls, they'd often played house on long Saturday afternoons. They always pretended they were married with families, living in far-off exotic places. But never in Cassie's wildest dreams had she imagined a setting like this, with a husband who looked like Trace, and children as adorable as Justin and Jason. If Susan could see her now...

"How nice to find my bride waiting for me." His deep, mocking voice startled her.

His bride? She whirled around in time to see Trace dive into the water and swim to the opposite end of the pool in a fast-paced crawl. Halfway back he stopped, treading water, and shook his head. In the near darkness she could just make out his dazzling white smile.

"Come on in. The water's perfect."

Even though he was some distance away, Cassie felt self-conscious as she removed her robe. "I love to swim, but I'm not very good at it."

"I usually swim early in the morning and again at night before I go to bed. Now we're married, we can work out together." Shivers raced over her body, because something in his tone implied that he expected her to join him on a regular basis and wouldn't take no for an answer. She couldn't understand why it mattered to him, since they'd be alone and there'd be no need to keep up the pretense. "It helps me unwind more than any sport I can think of." He looked at her a moment. "Are you about ready to jump in?"

She had just put a cautious toe in the water, bracing herself for the shock. But the temperature was so different from the chilly Pacific Ocean at Carmel, where she'd occasionally swum with Rolfe, it was as though she'd stepped into a bathtub. "I don't even have to get used to it!" she cried out in delight. "Gaugin was wrong. Paradise is right here!"

She heard Trace's deep-throated chuckle as she pushed off from the bottom step and swam to the other side, making sure she didn't get too close to him. On her third lap across, she felt a pair of hands grasp her around the waist and flip her onto her back.

"Trace!" she gasped, not only from the unexpected contact, but because he had taken her beyond the patio overhang and she found herself looking up into a blue-black sky dotted with brilliant stars.

"I'm not going to let you drown," he reassured her. "Lie there and relax, kick your feet. You're more rigid than Justin at his worst."

Only once did she venture a glance at his face. His skin was beaded with moisture and his black hair lay sleek against his head. She quickly closed her eyes again. She felt helpless and exposed with his gaze free to wander over her semiclad body.

It took all her control not to examine his hard-muscled physique with the same concentrated thoroughness. If she tried to move, her arm rubbed against his hair-roughened chest, reminding her how utterly male he was. Everything about him excited her. His size, his masculinity, his firmly carved mouth.

She came to the stunning realization that the bitter-sweet ache that seemed to be part pain, part ecstasy, was *desire!*

Susan had once tried to explain the sensation to her and had finally given up. But she'd insisted that Cassie would recognize it the moment she experienced it. She hadn't—until now.

Was this the way Rolfe had felt throughout their long courtship? If so, she had to admire his self-control. No wonder he grew more upset and moody each time she put off the wedding.

Without even trying, Trace had brought her alarmingly alive. From the first, he had accomplished what Rolfe had never been able to do. If she'd desired Rolfe like this, wouldn't she have wanted to get married as soon as possible?

Right now, she quivered with anticipation. She could hear every breath Trace took and feel the heat from his body sending a languorous warmth through hers. The longing to mold her soft curves against his solid strength was fast becoming a driving need.

Terrified that he could sense her desire and see the pulse throbbing in the hollow of her throat, she challenged him to a race. Without waiting for a response she catapulted out of his arms.

Of course he won. He waited for her at the far end of the pool with a rakish smile on his face. She touched the edge at least ten seconds after he did and drank in gulps of fresh air before bursting into laughter at her inelegant performance.

He studied her mouth intently, a gentle yet ironic smile curving his own lips. "Do you know that's the first time you've laughed with me when we've been alone? I like it."

Oddly embarrassed, Cassie sank down against the side of the pool until the water reached her neck. "As you've witnessed, I've got a long way to go to keep up with you."

His expression sobered. "I don't see our marriage as a competition, Cassie. What I'm hoping is that we'll share each other's lives. The children will grow up happier and healthier emotionally if they sense our marriage is a stable one. No one has to know what goes on—or doesn't—behind our bedroom doors except the two of us. Is that too much to ask? You don't dislike being with me, do you?"

Cassie was beginning to feel slightly hysterical. If he had any idea how much she didn't dislike being with him, he would run as far as he could in the opposite direction! Striving for composure, she smoothed several wet tendrils out of her eyes.

She didn't doubt his sincerity where the children's welfare was concerned. But now Cassie understood that his mother's fragile health had prompted him to enlist her cooperation in presenting a normal picture of married life to the rest of his family.

Her greatest problem would be to carry on a friendship, day after day, without ever betraying the

PLAY "MATCH 3"—WIN UP TO
A MILLION—$$$ IN LIFETIME INCOME (YES, $1,000,000!)
—GET FREE BOOKS & AN EXCITING SURPRISE GIFT, TOO!

★ Did you complete the first 3 rows of your "MATCH 3" Game? Did you print your name & address on the Game? Are you also playing & enclosing your Bonus Games? Please do, because so doing definitely qualifies you to win All Fabulous Prizes being offered, up to & including a MILLION—$$$ in Lifetime Income!

★ Did you complete rows 4 & 5? If you did, you are entitled to Free Books & a really nice Surprise Gift, as your introduction to our Reader Service. The Service does not require you to buy, ever. When you get your Free Books, if you don't want any more, just write cancel on the statement & return it to us.

★ You can of course go for prizes alone by not playing rows 4 & 5. But why pass up such good things? Why not win all the prizes you can – & why not get everything that's being offered & that you're entitled to? It's all free, yours to keep & enjoy. It's a "SURE FIRE" opportunity for you!

Use These Stamps
to Complete Your
"MATCH 3" Game

Simply detach this page & see how many matches you can find for your "MATCH 3" Game. Then take the matching stamps and stick them on the Game. Three-of-a-kind matches in rows 1 through 3 qualify you for Big Money Prizes—up to a Million—$$$…

…THREE-OF-A-KIND MATCHES IN ROWS 4 & 5 QUALIFY YOU FOR FREE BOOKS & A NICE SURPRISE GIFT AS WELL! PLAYING IS FREE – FUN – EASY & THE WAY TO WIN! *PLAY TODAY!*

physical side of her attraction for him. She finally said, "I admit it would be better for the children if they see us relating to each other as friends and companions."

Maybe she was mistaken, but she thought some of the tension eased out of him. "I'm glad you agree, because in two weeks the family's going on our annual skiing vacation to Snowbird, Utah, and I wanted to give you plenty of time to prepare for it."

She had that suffocating feeling in her chest again. "What about the children?"

"Nattie will take care of them."

"I see. How long will we be gone?"

"A week."

A week with Trace? Alone in the same room? She swallowed hard.

"Snowbird isn't the end of the earth, you know," he said harshly, his brows drawing together in displeasure. "You can phone the house every day to assure yourself the children are all right. If anything of a serious nature developed, we could be home in a matter of hours."

Cassie decided to let him go on believing that the children were her only concern. "You may as well know I've only been on skis twice in my life. I'm afraid I'd embarrass you on the slopes. Why don't I stay home with the boys and you go with your family? In fact, it might be a good time for Nattie to have a vacation, as well. She—"

"Either we go together, or we don't go at all!" he broke in angrily. Like quicksilver, his mood had changed. He suddenly shoved off for the opposite end of the pool, moving with tremendous speed. He was out of the water before she could call him back.

"Wait!" she cried out and swam after him, afraid she'd really alienated him this time. Unfortunately, she couldn't make it to the other end of the pool without stopping several times to catch her breath. She was terrified he would disappear into his own rooms, leaving her with everything still unresolved. "Trace," she gasped as her hand gripped the edge, "I was only trying to spare you. I ski like I swim."

He was toweling himself dry and slanted her a hostile look. "Do you honestly think I give a damn *how* you ski? Or even *if* you ski? I don't care if you lie around in the hotel bed all day watching television! From what I gather, for the last five years your life hasn't exactly been easy.

"Between Susan's and Ted's deaths, not to mention your mother's, a broken engagement and caring for Jason, you've had more to deal with than most people I know. And at the same time, you've been working all hours to earn a living. You don't seem to understand that I'd like to give you a chance to relax and play for a change, away from your work and the constant demands of the babies."

Her legs almost buckled at his unexpected explanation. Whenever she thought she had him figured out, he said or did something that increased her respect and made her care for him that much more.

A new ache passed through her body. She didn't *want* to care about him. She didn't want to worry about him—or think about him all the time. Lately she'd started fantasizing about what it would be like if he made love to her. Much more of this, and she'd end up an emotional wreck.

Her green eyes, wide with urgency, beseeched him to listen. "If I sounded ungrateful, I'm sorry. I suppose it's a combination of worrying about being away from the children for the first time and fear that you'll regret taking me along."

The expression on his face altered slightly as he held out her robe in invitation, but his eyes were still wary. As fast as she could manage, she clambered out of the pool and slipped her arms into the sleeves. His hands remained on her shoulders while she cinched the belt around her waist.

"You're an independent little thing," he whispered, kneading the taut muscles in her shoulders and neck. "It's time someone took care of you for a change."

She could feel the heat of his hands through the damp fabric. If he continued this, she was afraid of what she might do, afraid she'd embarrass them both. "You've spoiled me and Jason, and you know it, Trace. But I worry you've taken off too much time from your responsibilities at the bank, helping us move here and settle in. I wish there was something I could do for you in return."

His hands stilled for a moment. "There is," he muttered before removing them completely. Part of her was relieved he had broken contact, but another part craved his touch. Not trusting herself, she walked to the nearest lounge chair and sat down, making sure the robe covered her knees. This far from the pool, he was almost a silhouette in the near darkness.

"Tell me what's on your mind," she urged him.

He stood there holding both ends of the towel he'd slung around his neck. "You may not be an expert swimmer or skier, but your genius with needle and thread is nothing short of phenomenal. When I walked into your apartment with Jason that morning, I was overwhelmed by your talent and creativity."

A compliment from Trace meant more to her than the adulation of anyone else in the world. "Lots of women do what I do."

"Perhaps. But the finished product isn't always a masterpiece. I hope you won't be angry when I tell you I went through your apartment rather thoroughly, examining the goods, so to speak. Nothing bought for Justin in any store, anywhere, compares to the quality and originality I saw displayed in your apartment. I stand in awe of your accomplishments, Cassie."

"Thank you," she murmured shakily.

"I also felt like a fool for the callous way I suggested you move to Phoenix when I had no idea of the complexities involved in earning your livelihood." There was a slight pause. "Tell me something honestly. Is your work a labor of love?"

She couldn't help but wonder what he was getting at. "Long before I made any money at it, I loved creating an idea and seeing it through to completion. It's...something I have to do. When they find me dead, I'll probably be buried in batting, slumped over my sewing machine with a bunch of pins in my mouth.''

"Somehow I knew you'd say that." He chuckled. "You and Lena are kindred spirits.''

"I liked her very much, even after only one meeting.''

"Maybe you're the person who'll make the difference." The cryptic remark intrigued her.

"What do you mean?''

"You're both artists. You live in that elite world reserved for those who were born gifted.''

Cassie made a noise of dissent. "You can't seriously compare what *I* do to her talent!''

"I already have." His firm tone told her that to argue the point would be futile. "You make a child's world the most exciting, magical place on earth, just as it should be. Lena makes it possible for those of us who shove paper around to enjoy the breathtaking beauty of the desert without ever leaving our air-conditioned offices.''

"There's a certain genius in shoving paper around. Particularly *your* paper," she quipped. "Give me three days in your office and your entire family would find themselves without a business and no roof over their heads.''

The patio rang with his uninhibited laughter. "Well, since you brought up the bank, I have a proposition for you." Cassie sat forward, instantly alert.

"We lease properties, both residential and commercial. Right now, there's a studio vacant in Crossroads Square, an area of Phoenix that attracts tourists, as well as locals. By most standards it's not large, but it has four separate rooms with a cottage kind of feel, like you might see at a beach resort in Laguna or Balboa. It would be the perfect place to display your handicrafts. You need a showroom.''

She had been concentrating on the sound of his voice, and it took a minute before she actually heard his words. She jumped immediately to her feet. ''There's nothing I'd love more. It would be a dream come true, but I could never afford the rent, because I looked into the possibility in San Francisco and—''

''Don't jump to conclusions until you've heard me out,'' he cautioned before she could say another word. ''How much do you have saved from your Christmas sales after taxes?''

''About eight thousand dollars.''

''With that much money, you could sign a six-month lease.''

''But six months wouldn't give me enough time to fill it with inventory, and then I'd have no money to reinvest in materials and—''

She heard him make a sound of exasperation. ''Cassie, you said you wouldn't interrupt until I'm finished. Sit down before you wear out my patio with your pacing.''

''I'm sorry.'' With so much nervous energy to expend, she needed some form of movement. She found a spot at the edge of the pool and dangled her feet in the water, splashing gently. He wandered over to her and it was then that she noticed his right foot. Without thinking, she bent closer and touched it with her index finger. *"You have webbed toes, just like Jason!"* Her astonished cry rang out and she clapped a hand over her mouth at its loudness.

"A legacy from the Ellingsworth side of the family," he drawled in amusement. "Both of Mother's feet are similarly... afflicted."

"I wouldn't call it an affliction," Cassie argued. "When I first saw Jason's foot, I thought it was rather sweet. Susan and I investigated the medical records available in both Ted's and our family, but we couldn't find any mention of webbed feet. I guess that's when I started to take Susan's suspicions seriously."

"And your odd little duck turned out to be mine," he said, causing both of them to chuckle.

"Is that what convinced you he was your son?" She could still picture the expression on his face when he reached for Jason's tiny foot that first day in his office.

"No. I took one look at the shape of his body and his complexion. He had to be my son. The Ellingsworth webbed toes were just the final proof."

"And all the time I thought he was a Ramsey."

"Oh, I'm sure a little Ramsey is in there somewhere. But what's most important, he has you for a mother. You're a natural, did you know that?"

"Except I've been spoiling Justin, as you pointed out yourself."

"True, but no more than I've spoiled Jason," he replied with surprising honesty. "I admit I was somewhat hasty in judging you, especially since I've been equally guilty. However, I imagine time will remedy the urgency we both feel to make up for those lost months. And returning to your crafts work will put a balance back in your life. You've been missing that since you agreed to marry me.''

Again his perception and honesty surprised her. She'd been so preoccupied by her new responsibilities and her growing attraction to Trace, she hadn't yet found a moment to give serious thought to her business. ''Maybe a few years down the road I'll have enough money to look into the idea of opening a shop.''

''But that might be too late for Lena.''

Lena again.

''She needs someone outside the family who believes in her work and will encourage her to see it as a viable career. Someone who has validity in her eyes. I think you could be that person. You could infect her with your own interest. Your joy in what you're doing.''

What was he getting at? ''You mean like going into business with her? Opening a gallery with her art and my crafts?''

He nodded. ''Maybe you could call it something like The Mix and Match Gallery—in honor of the unusual way we met and became a family.'' There was a perceptible pause, then he asked, ''Does the idea appeal to you?'' She noticed the tiniest hint of anxiety in his question, as if her answer was important to him.

''*Appeal?*'' She jumped to her feet and gazed into his face, giving him a full, unguarded smile. ''It's a fantastic idea! In fact, why don't we call it Mix and

Match Southwest, since we'll be mixing and matching her art and my crafts and everything will have a southwestern theme?'' Her thoughts were tumbling excitedly over each other. ''We could have a logo with a cactus and maybe a setting sun or a coyote, and . . . oh, it'll be wonderful!''

His eyes kindled. ''You mean it? You wouldn't mind sharing space with her, provided she was willing? It would be predominantly your shop of course— at this stage, anyway. If necessary, I'll pay the rent for the second six months, only that would have to remain our secret. It seems to me that between the two of you, there should be enough profit to stay in business another year.'' He paused again. ''Would it make *you* happy, Cassie?''

When they'd begun this conversation, she thought he'd brought up the idea of a gallery solely for Lena's benefit. But the concern in his voice just now led Cassie to believe he was trying to please her, too, and that belief filled her with an all-consuming warmth. ''You know it would,'' she answered in an unsteady voice. ''Do you recall that watercolor at the top of the stairs? The one with the little Hopi girl standing next to those rocks at sunrise?''

He nodded. ''It's one of my favorites.''

''Every time I pass it, I itch to get out my sketch pad and design dolls and wall hangings based on that lovely child. In fact, living in this house has inspired me with the flavor of the Arizona desert. I've already planned out an area rug for my room, and the watercolor of the flowering cactus hanging in your office would look perfect next to it. Trace, for the opening I could use a Southwest theme with Lena's watercolors as the focal point!''

Before she could say anything else, he lowered his head and pressed his lips to her forehead. ''You have a generous nature, Cassie. I'm counting on you to win Lena over to the idea.''

Her heart hammered in reaction to his touch—and yearned for more. ''Maybe I could work up some items before we go to lunch next week and invite her back to the house. If she saw them arranged around the watercolors, it might excite her.''

''I'm sure it will, but getting her to make a commitment is something else again.'' A troubled look entered his eyes. ''In college she fell in love with her art teacher. They had an affair that ended when she walked into his apartment and found him in bed with another student.''

Cassie cringed at the all-too-common scenario.

''Considering that she thought they were getting married, that alone would have been devastating enough. But not satisfied with betraying her, he attacked her art and told her she was wasting her time. His final insult pretty well destroyed her confidence. He told her she'd never be more than a mediocre painter at best.''

''But anyone with eyes can see how brilliant her work is!'' Cassie insisted. ''When did this happen?''

''Twelve years ago. She hasn't done any painting since.''

"You mean the watercolors in your office and here at the house were all done while she was still in college? She was that good, even back then?"

"That's right," he said, tight-lipped.

"Her teacher probably recognized her talent and couldn't bear the competition. No doubt her work surpassed his. I've seen the same situation in the music department at the university where I studied piano theory. To think she let his rejection prevent her from working at her art all these years. It's tragic."

He nodded gravely. "Her husband, Allen, knows she'll never be completely fulfilled unless she gets back to her painting. He's done everything possible to encourage her but she refuses to even talk about it."

"The hurt must have gone very deep."

"It did. And to complicate matters, she feels insignificant around the family, overpowered by us. She's not like you, Cassie. She would never have fought me for Jason the way you did. You live by the strength of your convictions and don't let anything defeat you. You're practical and resilient—a survivor. You'd stand alone if you had to. If some of your confidence could rub off on Lena, it might change her life."

"I'm glad you told me about her," she said in a small voice. "I'll do what I can. Now if you don't mind, I'm very tired and I need to go to bed. Good night, Trace."

His whispered good-night followed her across the patio and up the stairs.

Though he obviously meant his remarks as a compliment, her spirits plummeted. Apparently she and his ex-wife, Gloria, had something in common, after all. They were both the antithesis of the fragile, helpless woman who aroused a man's undying love and brought out his instinctive need to protect and cherish.

The Joan of Arcs of this world would always be admired, but they would remain on their pedestals *alone....*

CHAPTER SIX

EXCEPT FOR A VISIT to the vacant shop in Crossroads Square and the subsequent signing of a year's lease, Cassie saw Trace only in passing during the next week. He explained that he had a backlog of work; as a result, he stayed at the office through the dinner hour every night so he could catch up before they left on their ski trip.

Cassie told herself she was glad his banking responsibilities kept him away from the house. Without his disturbing presence, she could simply relax with the children and sew at her own pace. Trace had helped convert the middle guest bedroom into a workroom. The light was perfect. Best of all, she was close to the children and could hear them when they woke up from their naps.

But to her dismay, Trace was continually on her mind. His energy and vitality, his handsome face and powerful body, made it impossible for her to concentrate fully on anything else. And when he was home, even if he was locked in his study or playing with the children, she was aware of him. No matter the hour, her pulse raced when she heard his car in the driveway. But what alarmed her even more was the disappointment she felt when he drove off to work each morning.

After five whole weeks of his attention and companionship, she discovered life wasn't nearly as exciting without him around. Always before, she'd been able to immerse herself happily in her work, unconscious of time passing. Now while she bathed and fed the children or cut out patterns, she often glanced at the clock, estimating how many hours it would be before he came home.

Lena called early in the week to make a date for lunch. Cassie put her off until Friday so she'd have enough time to work up several pieces that drew their inspiration from three of Lena's paintings. Trace brought home one she'd requested from his office. She used another two from the group hanging on the wall along the staircase.

In order to make the impact as striking as possible, she enlisted Nattie's help in converting the dining room into a sort of gallery. The effect was even more stunning than Cassie had imagined, because the room, with its arboretum of exotic desert plants, lent itself perfectly to the Southwest theme.

Though she kept her thoughts to herself, Cassie felt that something out of the ordinary had been achieved. She could hardly sit still through lunch with Lena, waiting for the moment they would go home.

If Trace's sister sensed Cassie's suppressed excitement, she hid it well. She asked dozens of questions and insisted on knowing all the details of Cassie's life and the events that eventually led her to Trace's of-

fice. Several hours later, when Cassie invited Lena
back to the house to see the children, Lena was still
chuckling over Trace's initial plan to have Cassie ar-
rested. But her laughter subsided when she caught
sight of her own watercolors displayed with Cassie's
creations in plain view of anyone standing in the living room.

Like a person walking through water, Lena moved
into the dining room. Cassie followed a few steps behind, uncertain of Lena's reaction and almost afraid
to breathe. Those paintings were associated with a
painful time in Lena's life. At this early stage in their
friendship, the last thing Cassie wanted to do was open
old wounds or create a rift between them. It was because she had Trace's blessing that she dared to in-
volve Lena at all.

Lena studied the arrangement in silence for a long
time. "Do you mean to tell me you've made all these
since you came to Phoenix?" she finally asked.

"Yes, except that they aren't completely finished."

"They're fabulous."

"Your paintings inspired them, Lena. I took one
look at your little Hopi girl and I could visualize her
adorable face on dolls and wall hangings and all sorts
of things. Every one of your paintings has given me a
dozen new ideas. I can't work fast enough to keep up
with them."

"Trace told me you were a genius with fabric."

"And I told him that whoever painted those scenes
in his office has incredible talent. Your work excites

me and makes me reach out for things I didn't know were in me. You know what I mean?''

Lena turned around and stared at Cassie. ''You really meant what you said the other night, didn't you?''

Taking a deep breath, Cassie answered, ''You already know the answer to that. Have I made you angry, using your paintings for inspiration without telling you?''

''Angry?'' Lena's gray eyes widened in surprise. ''I've never been so flattered in my life.''

Cassie's body went limp with relief. ''As you know, I've only ever sold out of my own home. At first I started making up dolls and stuffed figures from fairy tales and cartoons to help bring in a little more money. Pretty soon I was flooded with orders. I've sewn everything from frogs to princes. But I've never had a theme for my work or even considered it until I saw your paintings.''

Lena fingered her long braid absently. ''You obviously went to all this trouble—arranging everything so beautifully—for my benefit. Why?''

''Before I met Trace, I planned to open my own boutique in San Francisco as a showcase for my work. But everything changed when he asked me to marry him. Now that we're settled, I've used the profits from my Christmas sales to sign a lease on some space in Crossroads Square.''

''Crossroads Square?'' Lena mouthed the word wistfully, sounding very faraway. ''That's a perfect place if you want to attract the tourist trade.'' She stared at Cassie in puzzlement. ''Does Trace know about this? I-I thought you were going to stay home with the children."

"I do stay home. Every day. And I manage to enjoy the children and sew at the same time. How else do you think I could turn out so much work?" Cassie smiled mischievously. "But if I don't have a place to display and sell it, pretty soon Trace will have to build me a warehouse."

Lena burst into laughter. "You're a complete surprise, Cassie Ramsey."

"No." Cassie shook her head, liking the sound of her new name. "Just driven by a compulsion stronger than I am."

A shadow crossed Lena's face; she started to say something, then apparently changed her mind.

Cassie hesitated a moment, then decided to plunge ahead. "Lena, I have to admit I had ulterior motives in inviting you back to the house today. You see, I'm holding my grand opening in a month, and I need your permission to display the things I've already made. The fact is, I've copied your work and I really have no right to sell any of this." She gestured around the room. "Believe me, I'll understand if your answer is no. But as time is of the essence, I need to know how you feel . . . in case I have to get started on another theme entirely."

Picking up one of the dolls, Lena studied it carefully, then looked at Cassie, eyes brimming. "How could I possibly turn you down when you've done such exquisite work? It would be on my conscience forever."

Impulsively Cassie threw her arms around Lena in an exuberant hug. "I was praying you'd say that, because I can't think of another theme that could possibly work as well as this one. To be honest, I knew my opening would have to be unique in order to generate business. And when I saw your art, I was immediately drawn to it. I think other people would feel the same way."

In the heavy silence that followed her remarks, Cassie removed the paintings from the groupings of crafts, then leaned them against the far wall. Lena gazed at her uncomprehendingly, and Cassie had to bite hard on her lower lip to keep from smiling.

"Take a good look at everything without your paintings to show them off, Lena. The things I've made are nice in and of themselves, but the display falls flat, don't you think? Be honest now."

After another quiet interim, Lena nodded.

Crossing her fingers behind her back, Cassie ventured, "Would you allow me to use your paintings the way I've done here to open the show?" Without giving Lena a chance to respond, she rushed on. "I have to admit I've sketched out ideas for dozens of fabric crafts based on another ten of your paintings. If I work night and day, I can have everything ready for the opening. But without your art as a foil, I won't be able to achieve the same impact."

While Lena hesitated, Cassie quickly put the paintings back in place among the crafts for her sister-in-law's benefit. "You see? I'm right, aren't I?"

After a minute of studying the display, Lena nodded, looking slightly bemused. "Everything works perfectly together."

"Then you'll let me use them?"

"I'd be cruel if I said no."

"Thank you, Lena." Cassie couldn't help giving her another hug. "It's one thing to sell things out of your own home, and another to display them in a shop. I've been terrified at my own audacity. But with your paintings, I know the opening will be an eye-catcher."

Conscious of taking a calculated risk, Cassie added, "I noticed you haven't signed your paintings."

"No," came the quiet admission.

"I'm afraid you'll have to if I'm going to show them. Otherwise clients will assume I painted them."

Lena was examining the Hopi girl canvas, frowning in concentration. "I need to finish the detail on her dress if you're going to use this." She finally stood up and faced Cassie. "I'll tell you what. Ask Trace to bring home the paintings from the office you're planning to use. Next week I'll go to the art store for supplies and come over to sign them all."

"Don't you have materials at home?" Cassie asked, striving to remain unemotional when inside she was bursting with excitement.

"Heavens, no." She let out a bitter laugh. "I'm afraid my art career was very short-lived and I tossed everything out. In fact, I haven't touched a brush to canvas in years. When I worked on these paintings, I never dreamed anyone else would ever see them. I would have thrown them away, but Trace said he wanted them and offered me money to take them off my hands. Of course I wouldn't have let him pay me for junk.'' She sighed, shaking her head. ''My brother...''

''He believes in your work.''

Lena's gaze slid away. ''Well, now that I've committed myself, I'd better look over everything you plan to use. I might find other details that were left undone.''

''Lena, I can't thank you enough. To be frank, I've been frightened to tell you what I've been up to—particularly since I'm calling the shop Mix and Match Southwest. If you hadn't given your permission, I don't know where I would have turned for inspiration. Trace seems to believe in my work, as well. I—I want him to be proud of me.''

''In case you hadn't noticed, he already is,'' Lena said wryly. ''Of all my brothers, I feel closest to him, and I can tell you honestly that when Allen and I arrived at the party, Trace's eyes had a glow I've never seen before. Only you could have put it there.''

''That's because he's so crazy about Jason.'' She fought to keep the tremor out of her voice.

Lena eyed her shrewdly. ''Of course he is, but I saw the way Trace looked at you, the way he held on to you all evening. I've never seen him behave like that with any other woman.''

''Not even Gloria?''

''Especially not Gloria.''

Cassie wanted to ask more questions about Trace's former wife, but restrained herself; this wasn't the right time. "Trace's attention to me was solely for your mother's benefit."

"What does Mom have to do with how my brother treats you?" Lena asked in a perplexed voice.

"It's because of her heart condition. He wants her to believe our marriage is a love match."

"And it's not?" Lena burst out.

Cassie sucked in her breath. "Trace is grateful to me for uniting him with his son. But you might as well know he asked me to marry him and I accepted so neither of us would have to be separated from the children. I couldn't bear to lose them," she whispered.

"What?"

"Trace isn't in love with me, Lena. Ours is what people used to call a marriage of convenience. I can't go on pretending something that doesn't exist. At least not to you, because...because I want us to be friends."

"I do, too," Lena murmured, "but if you're telling me you're not in love with my brother, I don't believe you."

Lena's directness caught Cassie off guard and she felt heat rising to her cheeks. "None of it really matters, because Trace isn't interested in me that way. In fact, one of the conditions he set for our marriage was that both of us could see other people, as long as we were discreet."

"My brother said *that?*"

"Lena, we've never slept together. He's only ever kissed me once, the day we were married." Her voice trailed off as she recalled the thrill of it. Before Lena could respond, Cassie blurted out, "I can hear noises from upstairs. The boys must have awakened. I'll get them ready and bring them down."

Without waiting for a response Cassie raced from the living room and dashed up the stairs, thankful the babies had interrupted her painful conversation with Lena.

As Cassie changed their diapers, Nattie poked her head into the nursery. "Do you need help?"

"No. Jason seems to be a little off color, but I'm sure it's nothing. Since Trace won't be home for dinner, I can fix a simple meal for myself and the boys. So why don't you and Mike take the rest of the day off? You deserve a rest."

Nattie's face lit up. "You're sure?"

"I'm positive. Lena's going to stay a while and keep us company."

"All right. Thank you, Cassie. It's a joy to work in the same house with you."

"The feeling's mutual, Nattie. Go and have a good time."

When Nattie had left, Cassie dressed the boys and carried them downstairs to see their aunt. To her relief, Lena made no mention of their prior conversation and enjoyed getting to know Jason better while Cassie encouraged Justin to take a few steps. It wouldn't be long before he was walking on his own.

Jason, on the other hand, could crawl everywhere and went after anything he wanted with an unswerving certainty that reminded both women of Trace and sent them into gales of laughter. But, unusual for Jason, he soon tired and cried to be held.

Cassie and Lena spent the rest of the afternoon exchanging anecdotes about the children, but as the dinner hour approached, Lena declared that she had to go home and feed her starving horde. Cassie was reluctant to see her leave, but was growing concerned about Jason, who'd become irritable and weepy, despite his long nap. His forehead definitely felt warm to the touch.

She put Justin in the playpen, then walked Lena to the front door, carrying Jason in her arms. "I'll phone you as soon as Trace brings the paintings home from his office."

The other woman nodded. "Cassie, will you do me a favor and not mention this to anyone else in the family?"

"You mean about using your art for my opening?"

"Yes. I'd like this to be our secret, if you don't mind."

"Of course I don't. I'll tell Trace not to say anything, either."

"Good. It's just that I stopped painting years ago and, well, I just don't want to deal with everyone's speculations..."

Cassie put a hand on Lena's arm. "If that's how you feel, I understand. You have my promise."

"Thanks." Lena kissed Jason's cheek, then Cassie's. "We'll talk again soon. We'll be able to spend some time together during our trip to Snowbird, too."

Lena's unexpected warmth pleased Cassie. "Thank you for your help, Lena. It means more than you know."

Cassie had a feeling that her sister-in-law wanted to say something further—perhaps about her marriage to Trace. But Lena seemed to think better of it. As soon as she drove off, Cassie headed for the kitchen to get Jason a bottle of juice. Then she gave him a sponge bath to bring down his slight fever and put him back to bed.

But while she was taking care of him, her mind was on Lena. Though Cassie had obtained her permission to use the watercolors, it didn't mean she'd automatically begin painting again. Trace was right; Lena still sounded far too bitter over her ex-lover's rejection. She'd lost all her self-confidence and, even worse, belief in her own talent.

But she hadn't turned Cassie down, and that meant she'd taken the first, necessary step. Cassie couldn't wait to tell Trace. She listened for him all evening as she fed Justin and bathed him, then put him in his crib. Jason fell asleep almost immediately.

After turning out the nursery light, she went downstairs to put the crafts and paintings away and restore order to the dining room while she waited for Trace. Around eight she heard a car pull into the drive. Moments later, the sound of the back door opening told her he was home.

Cassie rushed to the patio to meet him, anxious to share her news about Lena. "I thought you'd never get here, and I have so much to tell you! Lena and I—"

His eyes looked warm and expectant, but the ringing of the telephone prevented further conversation. He reached for it, and Cassie sat down at the small table, silently admiring the blackness of his hair, the laugh lines around his eyes and mouth, the deepness of his voice.

By his clipped response she could tell the call had to do with bank business; she hoped it wouldn't detain him for the rest of the evening. He pulled out his pocketbook and jotted down some notes, then finally hung up. She was bursting to tell him her good news, but swallowed her words when she saw his dark expression. One phone call had transformed him into a remote facsimile of himself. He turned his head to stare at her broodingly.

"What's wrong, Trace?" she asked in alarm.

"That was Western Union with a cablegram for you from a Mr. Rolfe Timpson in Brussels. I told the operator to go ahead and read it." He tore the page from his pocketbook and handed it to her.

The hostility emanating from him troubled Cassie a great deal more than the paper in her hand. Her gaze was drawn to Trace's crisp handwriting. "Dearest Cass," it read, "I got your letter and I strongly feel we have to talk. We've loved for a lifetime and I don't ever see that changing. I'm coming back to the States next month to see you. I'll call you as soon as I arrive in Phoenix. My deepest love, Rolfe."

After all this time, Rolfe was coming to see her. She would always love him in a special way. But her response to Trace in the pool had revealed a truth that changed everything where Rolfe was concerned.

What was it Susan had said? That Cassie and Rolfe had never been apart and needed the separation to make things clear, one way or the other....

They were clear, all right.

Her eyes shifted from the paper to the man who'd taken her heart by storm and brought her body to glorious life. *Oh, Trace, if you only knew...*

"He wants you back," he said in a harsh tone, "but that's just too damn bad because you're married to me now, Cassie, and that's the way it's going to stay."

If she didn't know why he'd asked her to marry him, his angry pronouncement would have led her to believe he was starting to care for her.

"Whatever Rolfe has to say, I'd never leave you and the children," she said honestly.

"Don't take me for a fool, Cassie. Do you think I don't know the bond that exists between the two of you? The years invested? The intimacy you shared?"

"We weren't intimate in the way you mean," she confessed in a quiet voice.

His eyes blazed. "If you're trying to tell me you never slept together in all those years, I don't believe you."

"Nevertheless it's true. Mother had very conservative beliefs and raised Susan and me to save ourselves for marriage. She challenged us to be the only girls in the neighborhood who didn't know all there was to know about what goes on between a man and a woman. She promised us it would be a lot more fun and exciting to learn along with our husbands.''

He stared at her as if she was speaking a foreign language. ''What went wrong between you and Rolfe?''

She wanted to blurt out that she wasn't in love with Rolfe. That was what had kept her from marrying him. But she hadn't known it, not until she met Trace. And fell in love with him.

''We were engaged a long time. When he pushed me to set a wedding date, I couldn't, because I was still grieving over my mother. After Ted was killed, he pressed me again, but I was so worried about Susan I couldn't even consider marriage just then, even though I loved him very much. I don't blame him for finally getting fed up and breaking our engagement.''

''Is that when he left for Europe?''

''Yes. But none of it matters anymore. Trace,'' she began in an excited voice, ''I wanted to tell you about Lena. She—''

''Not now, Cassie,'' he interrupted tersely. ''I'm in the middle of a hellish merger and I'll be spending most of the night in my study.''

Not since that first day in his office had he ever been intentionally rude to her. Here she'd done everything in her power to show him the past was dead for her and he treated her like this! Even if things had been different and she'd wanted to see Rolfe again, did Trace honestly believe she'd walk out on him and the children? He would have to divorce her before she'd leave!

He turned abruptly and took the patio stairs two at a time. Cassie felt like throwing something at him. After he'd disappeared from view, she stood there for a few minutes to get her temper under control, then went upstairs herself. When she heard Jason crying she made a detour to the nursery. The minute she picked him up she realized why he'd awakened in such distress. He was burning with fever. One look at the rash covering his chest and neck dispersed all thoughts of the tense scene on the patio.

She quickly undressed him and headed for the bathroom, knowing she had to get his temperature down as fast as possible. The rash covering his chest was a brilliant pink, and she could actually feel the heat radiating from his body. She filled the tub with cool water and lowered him in. He began to scream uncontrollably. All of a sudden she heard Justin, who'd been awakened from a sound sleep, bellowing at the top of his lungs, too.

"Cassie? What can I do to help?" came Trace's voice over all the commotion.

Relieved he was there, she turned to him eagerly. "Jason's fever is so high he has a rash. There's a new bottle of infant's pain reliever in the other bathroom. Would you mind getting it?"

"I'll be right back. And Cassie, don't worry too much. Justin once had the same thing. It looks like roseola to me. A virus—extremely uncomfortable for them but usually no serious effects."

Cassie nodded her relief but begged him to hurry. She was finding it difficult to calm Jason, who hated the cool water and fought her in earnest. Soon Trace returned, crouching beside her as he unsealed the brand-new bottle of pain reliever and removed the dropper.

He'd rolled his sleeves to the elbow, exposing his tanned hands and arms with their smattering of dark hair. "You continue to sponge him and I'll get this stuff down his throat. It should reduce his fever within half an hour and make him feel a lot better."

She couldn't figure out how Trace could remain so composed when she was practically falling apart with anxiety. After several attempts, Trace finally managed the impossible.

The sight of him bent over the tub ministering to Jason's needs filled her with an indescribable tenderness, and her earlier anger evaporated completely. But Jason seemed to be furious with her, and although it wasn't really rational, she couldn't help fearing that he'd never forgive her for this.

"Don't look so worried, Cassie," Trace said. "Jason's going to be fine, and in two days he'll have forgotten all about tonight. He already seems better, don't you think?"

Cassie reached out to touch Jason's cheeks and forehead. Trace was right. He wasn't as hot and had quieted down considerably.

"You're going to get better. Mommy and Daddy are right here. You poor little darling. You're freezing!"

"That's the idea," Trace murmured, continuing to scoop the cool water over Jason's blotchy red neck and chest.

"Mama. Dada." Jason called both their names clearly, and Trace flashed her a look of such sweetness, her breath caught in her throat.

With her upper arm she brushed the tears from her cheeks and grasped one of the child's hands. "Just a few more minutes and Daddy will take you out of the tub, darling. It'll be over soon."

Jason began to cry again and tried to sit up. It seemed like an eternity before his father finally said, "I think this little guy has had enough for now."

As soon as Trace lifted him from the water, Cassie had a towel ready and wrapped him in it. Jason clung to Trace as they left the bathroom. Cassie thought he'd take the baby to the nursery, but instead he headed down the hall for the master bedroom. Over his shoulder he asked, "Cassie, will you please bring me the juice I saw in his crib? If I hold him on my bed for a while, maybe I can get him to drink it."

Cassie hurried into the nursery for Jason's bottle, as well as a fresh diaper and a light cotton quilt. Justin was standing up in his crib, crying hoarsely. "Just a minute, Justin. Here, darling." She handed him a stuffed pig. "Mommy'll be right back."

The only time Cassie had been in Trace's bedroom was once with Nattie, when they'd put some clothes away in his drawers. She'd certainly never entered it when he was home. But right now she didn't think of that. She swept inside and dashed over to the side of the bed where he lay sprawled out full-length, his tie off and his shirt unbuttoned halfway down his chest.

Jason lay in the crook of his arm staring up at his father, still whimpering a little but obviously content.

Trace took the bottle and offered it to Jason while Cassie changed his diaper and replaced the damp towel with the quilt. She and Trace exchanged relieved glances, as Jason drank thirstily, even holding the bottle by himself.

Unfortunately, Justin was still howling mournfully. Trace sent Cassie a humorous smile, and something in his expression made her feel they really were husband and wife, in every sense of the words. She had to fight the impulse to lean down a little farther and kiss his mouth.

"I'm going," she whispered. "I'll be in the other room if you need me."

"Not yet," he said softly. He lifted his free hand to her face, shaping the palm to the contour of her cheek. "I was inexcusably rude to you earlier. Tell me what happened with Lena. Did you get anywhere with her?"

"Yes. She's willing to let me use her paintings for the opening."

There was a brief pause. "You made a better start than I'd hoped for," he said. "When we get to Snowbird, I intend to show you my appreciation. With no worries and no children, I'll be able to concentrate on you for a whole week."

Excitement coursed through her veins. For the first time since their wedding, they were going to be alone together, and Trace sounded as if he was really looking forward to it. Of course, she knew he was motivated by concern for his sister and by gratitude for Cassie's help, but she hoped he was beginning to be aware of her as a desirable woman.

"It sounds wonderful." She purposely kept her voice low and steady for fear she'd reveal too much. She left the room immediately afterward.

With her skin still tingling from Trace's touch, she quieted Justin by picking him up and carrying him downstairs for a snack. Happy to be cuddled, he ate a graham cracker and gulped down some warm milk. A half hour later he was ready for bed.

After she'd settled him for the night, she went directly to Trace's room and tiptoed inside. As she took in the sight of Jason lying on his father's chest, her eyes moistened. Father and son were sound asleep.

Careful not to disturb them, she felt Jason's forehead; his temperature had gone down, just as Trace had predicted.

Unable to help herself, she let her gaze wander back to her husband, whose disheveled black hair made him look uncharacteristically boyish. For a few minutes she studied the lines of his strong, straight nose and mobile mouth, the way his dark lashes fanned out against bronzed cheeks. She stared at his arm, still protectively circling his son.

I love him, she thought. *I love him so much I can hardly bear it.*

Before she could do something foolish—like lie down next to him—she crept out the door and flew to her bedroom, where she could give way to her emotions in private. Trace would never know how excited she was to be going on this trip with him, how desperately she wanted to spend time with him alone. But she'd have to be very careful never to let him know how much she craved his touch. How much she craved not just gratitude and respect, but love.

Unable to sleep, Cassie pulled on a nightgown and robe and went to her workroom, where she could unleash her energy on an idea that had been unfolding in her mind.

Going to her files, she found the pattern she wanted and began cutting out fabric. Four hours later, a stuffed, six-foot alligator with black hair and calculating blue eyes lay on the floor watching her with a wicked grin. Across the tail she had stitched the word "Daddy."

When it was finished she opened the closet door and stood the alligator on end in the far corner. To make sure it remained hidden, she draped it with a swath of white canvas, then shut the door.

If Trace ever saw it, he'd know the truth. He'd know she was in love with him. Cassie couldn't imagine anything worse—because he wasn't in love with her. He'd feel only pity, and Cassie didn't think she could stand that.

CHAPTER SEVEN

"I'VE NEVER SEEN so much snow," Cassie gasped as the large airport limousine carrying the Ramsey clan approached the lodge at Snowbird. She was pressed between Norman and Trace, who kept his arm constantly around her; her joy was diminished, since she realized it was a show of affection for his family's benefit.

"Actually Utah's had a mild winter this year," Trace said in a low voice near her ear. "I can remember coming up here several times when there were literally walls of ice. The state's in a drought cycle right now."

She surveyed the towering white mountain peaks knifing through the thin, freezing cold air. "You'd never know it." She tried desperately to appear unaffected by his nearness, but her heart was hammering out of control. She didn't know if her disorientation was due to the altitude or to the fact that she'd be sharing a bedroom with Trace in a few minutes.

"I can't wait to hit the powder!" James announced as the limo pulled to a stop. "Last one out brings the skis for everybody."

"Oh, brother!" This came from his wife, Dorothy, who sat across from Jane, Norman's wife. Lena and Allen shared the front seat with the chauffeur.

A great deal of good-natured bantering went on as they proceeded to find their bags and carry in their ski equipment.

The heat generated by a roaring blaze in the giant hearth off the lobby welcomed new arrivals. Cassie wandered over to it while Trace dealt with registration. A jaunty-looking Lena gravitated to the fire with Cassie, sporting an all-navy ski outfit that suited her trim figure perfectly. Cassie, on the other hand, felt conspicuous, dressed in brand-new fluorescent-green ski bib and white, green and blue matching parka.

Several days after Jason had fully recovered from his roseola, Trace had purchased the outfit, along with skis and boots, and had brought everything home gift-wrapped. He made her open the packages the second he bounded in the house from work.

A card lying on top of the tissue had caught her eye. Gingerly Cassie picked it up and read: "You have my undying gratitude for being such a wonderful, caring mother to our sons. I hope this gift will convey in some small measure my appreciation for the way you've turned this house into a haven I love to come home to. You've more than kept your side of our bargain, Cassie. I hope to show my appreciation when we go to Snowbird. We'll have a week to ourselves—a chance for Cassandra Ramsey to feel a little indulged for a change! Trace."

The sincere sentiment had moved her. But his note didn't contain the words she wanted to read, to hear, above all others. The realization that Trace might never fall in love with her filled her with a sudden deep despair. She fought to keep a smile on her face as she thanked him for the presents. But knowing she couldn't keep up the pretense for long, she'd made an excuse to leave the room, claiming she wanted to phone Lena.

As she called her sister-in-law, she felt Trace's probing gaze and sensed a strange undercurrent that she found more than a little troubling. To her vast relief, Lena was home and Cassie launched into conversation about their ski trip with feigned enthusiasm.

Even when Trace left the room, she could still feel his strained reaction and wondered what had caused it. Maybe she hadn't sounded grateful enough. Or maybe he resented her talking on the phone the minute he came home from work.

Whatever the problem, for the next week Cassie had taken great pains to make their home the haven he'd mentioned in his note. In between her sewing activities, she went on a cooking spree and fixed delicious meals, preparing some of his favorite Southwestern dishes. But if anything, her actions seemed to increase the tension between them. The more she tried to please him, the more polite and remote he became. It reached the point that she'd actually dreaded their trip.

At least around the house, the children acted as a buffer. But now she'd be alone with a difficult husband for six whole days and nights. She wondered how she'd survive their vacation, or even *if* she'd survive.

"Well, well. Where did you come from?" a friendly male voice said directly behind her. Cassie turned around to confront what she considered the classic male ski enthusiast. He was athletically built, with light brown hair bleached by the sun and a tan that resembled leather. A confident smile revealed a splendid set of white teeth. The man simply exuded self-satisfaction.

"We're from Timbuktu," Lena unexpectedly blurted out in a brash tone meant to send him packing. But his confident smile didn't crack, and he continued to stare admiringly at Cassie.

"If you want some help with your technique, I'm your man. Name's Hank. You'll find me by the lift every morning. I give group and private lessons."

Cassie tried hard not to laugh out loud at the man's aggression, but she would never have responded as rudely as Lena had. She merely gave him a bland smile. "Thanks for the tip. If I decide I need instruction, I'll look you up."

"Great! In that terrific outfit, you'll be easy to spot."

"Our room is ready." Trace had found her and was looking every bit as disgusted as his sister with the other man's attention. Cassie hadn't heard that icy tone since the first day in his office, when he'd almost succeeded in having her carted off to jail.

An impish mischief made her green eyes sparkle as she said, "Trace, this is Hank, one of the ski instructors for the lodge. Hank, this is my husband, Trace, and his sister, Lena.''

"How do you do?" Hank put out a hand, which Trace was forced to shake. "Your sister says you're from Timbuktu. As I understand it, you don't get a lot of snow in that part of Africa."

Hank had a sense of humor, she'd give him that. There was a protracted silence. "That's right," Trace finally muttered, stone-faced. He glared at Cassie. "Are you ready?"

Swallowing hard, she said, "Whenever you are."

"Then let's go."

In the uncomfortable silence that followed, she turned to Hank. "It was nice to meet you."

Hank grinned. "I always enjoy meeting people from foreign places. See you around."

Suddenly Trace was ushering her from the foyer, his grip on her arm firm. Lena found her husband, and the four of them rode the elevator together.

"Hey, why so serious?" Allen questioned his wife. "Can you believe six whole days without the kids?" He swooped down and kissed the end of her cold nose. "Brrr," he joked, causing Lena to laugh, bringing her out of herself. "It looks like you need warming up."

Cassie averted her eyes, envious of their easy relationship and their intimacy. When the doors opened to the fourth floor, she couldn't get out of the elevator fast enough and, apparently, neither could Trace.

"See you at dinner," they called out before the doors closed again.

Trace led the way to their room, which overlooked the snowy Wasatch Mountains where they'd be skiing. The afternoon sun glistened off the dazzling white peaks, making her eyes sting.

"I can't believe we're here. Only this morning I was looking out at the desert from the nursery window."

"And wishing you didn't have to come?" he asked grimly.

Cassie whirled around in surprise. "Why do you say that?"

"I'm not blind, Cassie. I saw the way you clung to the children this morning. Anyone would've thought I was dragging you off to—" he paused "—Timbuktu for a year, instead of a short holiday. Since I know you're dying to find out if they're still alive, I'll go downstairs and bring up the rest of our things while you phone home for a report."

He left the room before she could refute his words. But in all honesty, what was there to say? She *had* been dreading this trip, but not for the reasons he imagined. Snowbird had to be one of the most romantic places on earth—and it served as a painful reminder of the mockery of a marriage to a man who didn't love her.

Her gaze strayed to the two queen-size beds. She felt a wave of humiliation. Trace couldn't possibly feel any desire for her or he wouldn't have arranged for a room with two beds. Who in the family, except Lena, could guess that for the next week, Trace and his wife would be roommates, nothing more?

Hot tears spilled down her cheeks, but she quickly dashed them away with her hands. At home, when she grew frustrated over her futile love for Trace, she could escape to her sewing room or the nursery. But now that they'd arrived at the lodge, she had to make the best of an almost intolerable situation. She could think of only one thing to do. Ski!

Perhaps in six days she could learn the basics of a sport Trace loved. But she'd need lessons from one of the instructors—and judging by Trace's reaction, it had better not be Hank. Cassie disliked that type of obsessively flirtatious man, anyway. Perhaps there was another instructor available, one more interested in skiing than in the female skiers!

With an actual plan, Cassie felt a little better. She phoned the house in Phoenix, and Nattie put her mind at rest, assuring her the children were fine. She urged Cassie to forget everything and concentrate on Trace.

When she replaced the receiver, Cassie found herself wondering if Nattie's last comment was meant to be taken as a piece of womanly advice. The housekeeper knew Cassie and Trace slept in separate bedrooms. She probably found their relationship unnatural. *Well, so did Cassie!* But there didn't seem to be a thing she could do about it.

"Are they still breathing?"

Trace's biting sarcasm jolted her out of her reverie. She turned around, counting slowly to ten before answering. Somehow she had to salvage this trip; she had to get on better terms with her husband—who at the moment looked far too attractive for her peace of

mind. The gray-and-black-striped ski sweater complimented his dark good looks and emphasized his trim,
powerful build.

"The children are fine, and you're right. I've doted
on them to the exclusion of too many other things.
Maybe it's because I'm not their natural mother, so
I've taken on a greater sense of responsibility than is
warranted. Please believe me when I say I'm happy to
be here."

At her words, the stiffness seemed to leave his taut
frame and he moved closer. His eyes searched her face
for endless minutes. "Cassie, I realize you led a completely different life until you married me, and I've
expected far too much, too soon. Chalk it up to my
boardroom tactics." With a slow smile that made her
heart turn over, he put his hands on her upper arms.
"For the rest of this week, could we pretend there's
just the two of us and enjoy a vacation we both badly
need?"

"I'd love it."

"Good," he whispered, then leaned forward to kiss
the top of her head. Maybe it was her imagination, but
she thought he buried his face in her hair an extra-long
moment before lifting his head. Her body seemed to
dissolve with desire. The slightest contact triggered a
physical response she couldn't control, and she wondered if he could tell what his nearness did to her.
"Are you hungry?" he asked as he stepped back, re-
leasing her arms.

"Starving.

"Let's grab a hamburger. Then I'll take you out on the bunny hill and teach you a few fundamentals. In a day or two, you'll be ready to go up on the lift."

Cassie would willingly have gone anywhere with him. And since he'd offered to give up his own skiing time to teach her, she could hardly refuse.

The rest of the day Cassie reveled in his company. She alternated between fits of laughter and spills in the snow—with the occasional success—as she tried to master the snowplow and the art of falling down safely. If Trace thought her a lost cause, he didn't say so. But she'd never seen him smile so much, which gave her more pleasure than she dared to admit, even to herself.

As the sun started to go down, he grew more playful and began tossing snowballs at her. She tried to escape, but her skis crossed and she fell headlong into the snow. When he saw her predicament, he took off his own skis and scooped up a fresh handful of snow. She struggled onto her side and giggled as he started toward her with a predatory gleam in his eye.

"No, Trace!" she screamed through her laughter, trying to shield her face. With one gloved hand he easily caught her wrists and pinned them in the snow above her head, leaving the other free to begin his torture.

"Be kind," she pleaded on a shallow breath, her eyes half dancing, half fearful, as she met his gaze, which darkened in intensity the longer they stared at each other.

"My words exactly."

A moan trembled on her lips at the passion in his husky voice. The blood surged through her veins as he lowered his head and found her mouth with his own, creating an aura of scorching heat despite the near-zero temperature of the air. Each kiss grew deeper, hungrier. Cassie could no longer contain her own frantic response. When he wrapped her in his arms and pulled her against him, she feverishly kissed him back, losing all sense of time and place.

"Good grief, Trace. You've got a perfectly good room at the lodge for that sort of thing. I think you'd better take a run with us and cool off, little brother."

Norman's teasing voice penetrated Cassie's rapture, and she pulled sharply away from her husband. Not only was she more embarrassed than she'd ever been in her life, but to be so rudely transported back to reality made her want to weep with frustration.

With enviable aplomb, Trace got to his feet, then helped her up and handed her the ski poles she'd dropped. Cassie couldn't recover her own composure as quickly. She had to support herself with her poles so she could stand upright while she faced Trace's two brothers, who stood there unashamedly grinning at her. She didn't dare look at Trace. At this point he could be in no doubt that his wife more than welcomed his lovemaking.

She heard him ask, "Hasn't the lift closed yet?" When James said there was time for one more run, Trace turned to her. "If you don't mind, Cassie, I'll go with James and Norman and meet you back at the lodge for dinner."

What was going on? He seemed to be relieved that his brothers had interrupted their lovemaking; he'd leapt at the chance to join them. Yet Cassie could have sworn he was as shaken as she was by the passion they'd just shared. She'd thought he would tell his brothers to ski without him, that he and Cassie had other plans.

What a fool she was!

Trace was a man of experience and he'd simply been having a little fun in the snow. He hadn't meant anything serious. Most likely he was already regretting their interlude, because he hadn't expected her to respond the way she had. Well, she'd make sure he wouldn't worry that she'd gotten the wrong idea!

Lifting her head, she smiled brightly at the three of them. "To be honest, I was hoping someone else would come along to entertain Trace. For the last while, I've been dying to take my poor aching body back to the room and have a long hot soak in the tub. The altitude has made me so tired, I think I'll have a quick sandwich and go to bed. By the time you return, I'll probably be out like a light until morning."

"You sound like Dorothy," Norman moaned.

Trace's expression became shuttered, as if her answer displeased him. She couldn't figure him out. "I'll see you later then," he murmured, turning abruptly to get his skis.

With an aching heart Cassie watched until the three of them disappeared over the crest of the beginners' hill. He didn't once look back or wave.

What did he want? Should she have begged him in front of his brothers? Begged him to stay, to keep up the pretense that they had a normal marriage? If he hadn't regretted those intimate moments in her arms, then why had he left her?

Cassie didn't know what to make of his erratic behavior. Vowing never to get into such a vulnerable situation again, she trudged back to the lodge, ate another hamburger and went up to their room. An hour later, she climbed out of the tub, almost overcome with lethargy. She searched for the red flannel nightgown she'd made especially for the trip and fell into bed, exhausted. Once under the covers, she let out a deep sigh and was aware of nothing more until she wakened early the next morning, suffering from hunger pangs and sore muscles.

She glanced at her watch, surprised she'd slept so long. Trace was in the other bed, still asleep. When had he come to bed? She could hear his deep even breathing and noticed a tanned arm and shoulder above the blankets.

Carefully she turned on her side to watch him. Everything about him enthralled her. If he only loved her and she could be sure of his welcome, she'd climb in beside him right now and kiss him awake. The longer she gazed at him, the deeper her yearning.

When she couldn't bear it any longer, she slipped out of bed and hurried into the bathroom to dress. Now was as good a time as any to start ski lessons. Maybe later in the day Trace would join her again and she'd be able to show some improvement.

As quietly as she could, Cassie left the room and went down to the lobby to eat breakfast and arrange for lessons. Fortunately there was a woman on the ski patrol who taught group lessons in the morning before the lift opened, and Cassie signed up with her.

The class contained both children and adults at various stages of proficiency. Cassie discovered that Trace had taught her well, because she could keep up with the best of them. When the lesson was over, she hurried back to the room to tell him, but he'd already gone.

The rest of the day brought little pleasure. The flirtatious instructor, Hank, saw her on the hill later in the morning and wanted to ski with her, but she refused. Then it was time for lunch. She joined Dorothy, Jane and Lena, who all declared they'd had enough skiing for one day. Apparently the men had gone off together, so the women decided to play cards in front of the fire. Trace didn't make an appearance until everyone gathered for dinner in the main dining room that evening.

He greeted Cassie with a kiss on the cheek as if nothing was wrong, and laughed and joked with the others. Everyone described the day's events; inevitably, one of the women brought up the fact that Cassie had had a ski lesson. Trace murmured something appropriate and said that when she felt ready, they would take a run together. On the surface his behavior appeared perfectly normal. But Cassie sensed his withdrawal.

As the evening wore on, the family stayed downstairs for the musical entertainment. Cassie couldn't enjoy it because, although Trace always acted the part of a polite, concerned husband, he had distanced himself from her. This, more than anything, convinced her he wanted to forget what had happened on their first day in the snow.

Pleading fatigue, one by one each couple headed up to bed, until finally Cassie was left alone with Trace. "You seem tired," he said in that same polite voice. "Why don't you go up to bed? I'm going to have a drink in the bar."

Nothing could be plainer than that! Cassie murmured a good-night and barely made it to the room before she broke down sobbing. She couldn't take it much longer.

The next day started out like a repeat of the previous one, with Trace still sleeping soundly in the other bed as she left for her lesson. She was still agonizing over Trace when she entered the lobby afterward. Lena was waiting for her and asked if she'd like to take a shuttle bus down to Salt Lake City to do some shopping. Allen's birthday was the next weekend and Lena wanted to get him something special. Cassie didn't have to think twice about accepting her invitation. She wasn't an enthusiastic shopper, but anything was better than spending the rest of the day on the slopes hoping she'd run into Trace, or worse, praying in vain that he'd come to find her.

Lena wanted to keep their expedition a secret, so Cassie left Trace a note saying only that she was going down the canyon. They left the lodge with a group of other people to do a full day's shopping and sightseeing. The first thing Cassie bought was postcards, and while she and Lena ate Mexican food at Chef Trujillo's, she wrote short notes to some of her friends in San Francisco, including Beulah.

They spent the afternoon trailing in and out of shops. Cassie found hand-knit toques and mittens for the boys, some gourmet preserves for Nattie, and a small bottle of Canadian rye for Mike.

She managed to buy a gift for Trace, too. Quite by chance she'd seen a framed photograph of the mountains around Snowbird in a tourist shop, where Lena had already found another snow scene for Allen's gift. The shot was quite spectacular, with the early-morning rays tinting the snow-covered peaks. Luckily it didn't cost a great deal and was something she could buy with her own money, but she thought he'd like it.

By the time their bus pulled up to the lodge in the evening, the family had eaten and gone their separate ways. Cassie hurried upstairs with her packages, anxious to give Trace his present. But he wasn't in the room. If he'd gone to the bar, presumably he wanted to be alone, and she had no intention of disturbing him. If he was visiting with one of his brothers, she was equally unwilling to intrude. Dejected, she took a shower, put on her flannel nightgown and climbed into bed with a recent mystery novel she'd bought that afternoon.

Trace walked in half an hour later. Slowly Cassie's gaze lifted to his above the pages of the book. As always, she was achingly aware of him. He was dressed in sweats, with a deep tan that attested to a day's skiing—she noticed that instantly but she also noticed the tension in his posture and expression. "Hello," she said in an unsteady voice.

"So you're back." Grimacing, he tossed the room key on the table. "Did you have a good time?"

Cassie sat up straight, anxious to tell him about her day, to hear about his. "Yes. And I bought something for you. It's there on the bed."

He moved slowly to the bed and unwrapped the gift. "It's beautiful, Cassie—but you don't have to bribe me into going home. I know you never wanted to come to Snowbird in the first place."

The book fell out of her hands. "I don't want to leave. I'm having a good time."

His expression grew bleak. "Well, I'm not. I brought you here to spend time with you. But every time I turn around, you're missing. The family is beginning to wonder what's going on."

Anger made her face feel hot. "I thought the purpose of this trip was to be by ourselves and do what we wanted. If you remember, *you're* the one who took off with your brothers the first night we were here." She could have bitten her tongue for referring to that evening, but it was too late now.

Trace's mouth hardened, as if he didn't like being reminded of the incident. "Did you go to Salt Lake City alone?"

Cassie averted her eyes. His unexpected question had conveniently changed the subject. "No."

"I didn't think so."

Throwing back the covers, she got out of bed to face him. To her dismay, his eyes traveled unhurriedly over her curves, which weren't hidden by the red fabric, then finally lifted to her flushed face. It was almost enough to make her forget what they were arguing about.

"In case you're thinking I was with that ski instructor," she said calmly, "then you couldn't be more wrong. For your information, I went to Salt Lake City with Lena—at her request. I thought you'd realize she and I were together. She wanted to buy something special for Allen's birthday and didn't want him to know about it."

"Be that as it may, your disappearances have pretty well let the family know that your interests lie outside your marriage."

"That's unfair!" she cried. "How can you say such a thing? Except for the first day, have you ever asked me to ski with you? Have you invited me out to dinner? Did you ask me to stay with you in the bar and dance?"

His expression was tight with fury. "After hearing you tell my brothers you were hoping someone else would come along to entertain me, I had doubts that any invitation of mine would be welcome."

Cassie's eyes closed tightly. "I only said that so you wouldn't feel obliged to stay with me. I know how much you love to ski with them."

They stood facing each other in silence, like adversaries. Finally he said, "Whatever the reasons for our misunderstandings, this trip isn't working out. Be packed and ready to go in the morning.''

He placed the photograph and its crumpled wrappings on his night-table with a deliberate care that confused her. Then he disappeared out the door, leaving Cassie furious—and heartsick.

CHAPTER EIGHT

AFTER EATING a bit of the chicken salad a surprised Nattie had left for her, Cassie started up the stairs to check on the children, whom she'd put to bed earlier. As she reached the first landing, she heard the phone ring. She fervently hoped it was Trace. He'd left for the office after they'd returned from Snowbird that afternoon and hadn't bothered to come home for dinner. She dashed into his study, picked up the receiver and said a nervous hello.

"Cassie? It's Lena!"

"Lena? What are you doing calling me from Snowbird?"

"More to the point, what are you and Trace doing back in Phoenix? Allen and I decided to sleep in this morning. When we got up, James told us you and Trace had left the lodge to go home. Something about a problem with one of the boys. I think everyone else believed it, but I don't. Can you talk, or is Trace around?"

"He went to the bank to see if there was anything pressing. I put the children to bed an hour ago and just had some supper."

"Then you can talk. What's wrong? You know I'd do anything for you and Trace."

"You shouldn't have said that." Cassie swallowed back a sob. "Trace and I have had one misunderstanding after another," she said hopelessly.

"Which one of you called off the rest of your vacation, or am I being too nosy?"

"Of course not. If you want the truth, I think he's tired of having to pretend everything's perfect with us when we're around the family. I never seem to be able to say the right thing. We do much better alone at the house, with just the children. Our marriage won't survive another vacation."

"I'm sorry, Cassie. This must be so hard for you. I was once in love with someone and I thought he loved me, until I learned the truth the hard way. It took me a long time to get over him, so I can just imagine what you're going through right now. I wish there was something I could do to help."

"I appreciate your support and friendship. Unfortunately no one can make Trace fall in love with me," Cassie said in a voice that quavered despite her effort to sound matter-of-fact. "If it hasn't happened by now, it never will. That's the reality and I'm going to have to live with it. Don't forget, I went into this marriage for the children's sake."

"But the children will never be enough now."

"I hope you're wrong," she said softly, then broke off when she heard footsteps on the stairs. "Lena, I'll have to hang up. I think Trace is home."

"All right. I'll call you as soon as we get back."

"Thanks for everything." Cassie put down the receiver as the study door flew open and Trace stood there, silhouetted in the light from a hallway lamp. Cassie muttered a greeting, but something in his stance made her unaccountably nervous.

"You're upset. Did something go wrong with the merger while we were on our trip?" she asked.

"If you weren't so preoccupied with your phone call, you would have been able to hear the boys crying. Who has such a claim on your time you've been neglecting them?"

His unfair accusation stung Cassie to retaliation. "How dare you say that to me when you didn't bother to come home for dinner to be with them—or even call to let me know you'd be late!" she demanded, her chest heaving with indignation.

His hands curled into fists, and without volition, her eyes took in the strength of his body, the powerful thighs in tight-fitting jeans, the black knit shirt that clung to his chest like a second skin. They were close enough that she could feel the warmth of his body and smell the soap he'd used in the shower. Right now she couldn't think or move as desire for him engulfed her like a sudden burst of flame.

"I dare because I'm your husband." A hand shot out and grasped her wrist, bringing her closer and making her far too conscious of his body. "You still haven't answered my question."

She could have told him the truth—that it was Lena on the phone—but she didn't. She was too angry, because he didn't seem to trust her. And at the same time she needed to put distance between them before she lost complete control.

"As I recall," she said coldly, "*you* were the one who said what we did with our private lives was our own affair, as long as it didn't hurt the children. I never question the unorthodox hours you keep, and I'm not doing anything you haven't done since the day we were married." She tried to pull away, but he held her fast.

"And just what is it you think I've been doing?" he whispered. "Making secret assignations behind your back? Why should I do that when I have a wife who seems perfectly capable of filling everyone's needs— but mine? I think it's time you took care of them."

In the next instant he drew her into his arms and found her mouth with a savagery that made nonsense of her efforts to resist. For so long she'd wanted him, but not like this, not angry and suspicious of her motives. Yet she wasn't prepared for the intimate caress of his hands against the skin of her back, where her blouse had separated from her jeans. His touch softened and Cassie melted against every line and angle of his hard body, helplessly yielding to the seductive pressure of his mouth, his hands.

Cassie hadn't ever known this kind of ecstasy before, and she didn't want Trace to stop. Her arms slid around his neck so she could get even closer. She wanted to give, and go on giving until he knew in every single cell of his body that she loved him. That she always would.

Perhaps it was her moan of pleasure that caused a shudder to pass through his body. The next thing she knew, he had thrust her away from him. She cried out in surprise and clung to his desk to prevent herself from falling.

The faint light made it impossible for her to see his expression clearly. But if his shallow breathing and the tautness of his body were any indication, he'd been equally disturbed by their passionate embrace.

Then she heard a muttered curse before he blurted out, "I had no right to lay a finger on you, Cassie, let alone demand an accounting. Whatever you do with your free time is none of my damn business. I'm the one who's broken the rules of our contract and I swear it won't happen again. Why don't you go on up to bed. I know you're under a lot of pressure, getting ready for your opening. I'll lock up and take a look at the boys before I turn in."

She watched him leave the study and ached to call him back. But without knowing how he really felt about her, what he really wanted from her, she didn't dare. Living in the same house day after day had made them aware of each other to the point of physical need. She'd felt Trace's desire for her. But that didn't mean he was in love with her.

Drained from the explosive emotions, Cassie followed his suggestion and went to bed. But she was plagued with insomnia. Trace had set her on fire, exposing the primitive, womanly side of her nature, changing her preconceived notions about physical love for all time.

By two o'clock, her body was still reliving the taste and feel of his mouth and she couldn't fall asleep. Disgusted with herself, she went to her sewing room, where she immersed herself in work and didn't come out until seven in the morning.

When she went downstairs to start breakfast, she discovered that Trace's car wasn't in the driveway. He'd deliberately left the house early; when she realized this, her hurt intensified. She went through the motions of her morning routine, which included bathing and feeding the children. At noon Nattie took over so she could leave the house and drive to the gallery with as many things as she could load into the station wagon. This set the pattern for the next few days.

Besides all the new crafts she'd been making, she decided to sell all the stock items from her inventory, too. There was a second display room, which would be perfect. But even with Mike's help, it took several days to move everything from the house to the shop. During that time, she saw next to nothing of Trace, who came home too late to do more than kiss the boys good-night and disappear into his study.

On Friday, as Cassie was unpacking another set of freestanding shelves at the shop and trying not to think about the impossible state of affairs between her and Trace, Lena walked in, carrying some paintings.

Cassie stared at her sister-in-law. "I'm so glad you're back."

"I bet you thought I'd deserted you, staying so long at Snowbird, but Allen and I had to be alone. I've

tried to make up for lost time today by signing the rest
of the paintings. As you know, my car won't hold
more than two at a time, so I'll have to make several
trips.''

Shaking her head, Cassie said, ''We'll go back to the
house in the station wagon and get the rest. Now that
you've finished them, I'm going to stay here all evening and set up as much as I can to view the full effect.'' She glanced around. ''I think I'm going to have
to buy some more plants, though.''

Lena scrutinized everything with her artist's eye.
''I'll tell you what. I want to be home with the children for dinner. Then I'll come back here to help, but
it'll have to remain our secret. Allen can think I've
gone to a PTA meeting.''

''Are you sure?'' Cassie cried out excitedly. Trace
would be overjoyed if he knew how involved Lena had
become with Mix and Match.

''You're a remarkable woman, Cassie, but even I
can see how much work still has to be done.''

''The opening's coming up much too soon,'' Cassie agreed, ''and there aren't enough hours in the day
to accomplish everything. Now let's go home and get
the rest of the paintings.''

She didn't particularly relish the prospect of being
at the shop alone at night and would be thankful for
Lena's presence. Although she wasn't entirely comfortable with her sister-in-law's apparent penchant for
secrecy, she could understand it, too. Lena was so ter-
ribly unsure of herself and of her talent.

As it turned out, Lena and Cassie worked side by side for the next two nights, attempting to set up the most appealing displays possible. And they shared more confidences. Cassie marveled at her sister-in-law's decorating sense and thanked her repeatedly before they parted company Saturday night.

"Don't forget Allen's surprise birthday dinner at seven tomorrow. I phoned Trace earlier and invited him, so he knows you're both expected."

And probably dreading another evening with me in front of his family, Cassie mused painfully. "Will everyone be there?"

"No. It's just going to be the four of us," Lena explained, lessening Cassie's anxiety somewhat.

The next morning didn't begin well. Nattie informed Cassie that Trace had left to keep a golf date with a business acquaintance. When he did come home, he spent some time with the children, and she didn't see him until they were ready to go to Lena's.

They behaved civilly to each other, but during dinner Trace couldn't have been more distant with Cassie, more removed from her emotionally—a fact Lena was quick to observe. While they cleared the table, she flashed Cassie a look of commiseration.

Cassie was grateful for Allen, whose conversation as he opened his presents provided the only comic relief. His eyes met his wife's as he unwrapped the framed photograph she'd bought him in Utah and he sent her a message of love so fervent that Cassie lowered her own eyes. She knew he must be remembering the private time he and Lena had spent at Snowbird.

But the moment was brief and he quickly moved on to the other gifts, ending with Cassie's. Lena had told her that Allen loved to barbecue, so Cassie had made him a chef's apron embroidered with French cooking terms.

"So tell me, you lucky cuss." Allen poked Trace in the ribs. "How did you manage to end up with Cassie? She can cook, sew, she's a great mother and her skiing's coming along nicely. She's a looker, too."

Normally Cassie would have been amused by Allen's remarks. But she was too sensitive to Trace's mood just now. She found herself waiting uncomfortably for one of his carefully worded responses while she pretended interest in the birthday cake.

"You left out the part about her being a savvy business woman," Lena interjected on cue, saving Trace from having to utter a word.

"That's right," Allen murmured. "How's the shop coming?"

His question was directed at Cassie, but it was Trace who answered. "Judging by the nights she's stayed up sewing, I'd say she probably has more than enough things to fill several shops." Although his comment sounded innocent, Cassie wasn't deceived. She lowered her head, but not before Lena had sent her a sympathetic glance.

"When's the opening?" Allen asked, seemingly ignorant of the undercurrents. "Lena and I plan to be there."

"Next Saturday," Cassie said faintly. The tension emanating from Trace left her so nervous, she was finding it more and more difficult to speak.

Suddenly Lena cleared her throat and looked nervously at her husband. "Darling, I think it's time I made a confession." There was an air of expectancy after her announcement.

"We're not pregnant again, are we?" he teased, but Cassie could see the love shining in his eyes.

"No." Lena laughed. "When I told you I had meetings the last two nights, I was lying." Allen's smile slowly faded. "Actually, I've been helping Cassie at the gallery."

Allen blinked. "That's great. But why didn't you just say so?"

"Because... Cassie's using some of my old paintings as part of her display. At first I didn't want you to know about it because..."

He stopped eating his cake and gazed at his wife solemnly. "Does this mean what I think it means?"

She took a deep breath. "It means that I've been a fool to be so sensitive about the past."

"Honey..." Allen's hand grasped hers.

Something was going on here that Cassie didn't quite understand. Allen seemed overwhelmed with emotion. She automatically glanced at Trace and discovered his eyes focused on her, sending her a private message of gratitude. Even if the warmth in his regard had everything to do with her influence on Lena, Cassie basked in his approval. She had no pride anymore. She loved him too much.

In the background she could hear the phone ringing and then Becky, Lena's daughter, poked her head around the dining-room door. "Aunt Cassie? Uncle Trace? Nattie says you'd better come home. Jason woke up croupy."

The twelve hours following Lena's dinner party would have been a nightmare for Cassie if Trace hadn't been there to help nurse Jason through the night. First roseola, now a croupy cough that kept them all awake. By noon the next day, however, he seemed much better and Cassie finally relaxed.

She couldn't say the same for Trace. Fatigue lines etched his face from hour after hour of walking the floor with Jason. Cassie urged him to call Mrs. Blakesley and cancel any appointments for the day so he could go to bed. But Trace insisted he had to be at the bank for an important afternoon meeting and left the house at a run.

Once again she found herself marveling at the extraordinary strength of the man she'd married. Trace was unfailingly responsible, always dependable. The longer she lived with him, the more Cassie realized how much she, as well as others, particularly his family, relied on him. Though the youngest Ramsey, it was no accident that his brothers had made him chairman of the board. His confidence and his abilities made people put their trust in him.

Because he worked so hard, Cassie was concerned about his not getting enough rest, and she spent the remainder of the afternoon and evening worrying about her husband instead of Jason, who was starting to behave more like himself again.

Cassie had been asleep for some time when she heard a knock on her door. Alarmed, she glanced at the bedside clock, which said it was after midnight. The knock sounded again.

"Nattie?" she called anxiously and sat up in bed.

"It's Trace, Cassie. I need to talk to you. May I come in?"

"Yes. Of course." Her voice shook as she turned on the lamp and pulled the covers to her chin. "Is Jason bad again?" she asked as he entered her bedroom wearing his bathrobe. He must have come from the shower because the clean scent of soap wafted in the air.

Trace closed the door behind him and approached her bed. "No. I just checked on him. He's fine. So's Justin."

She swallowed hard. "When did you come home? I held dinner until nine, then put yours in the fridge."

"I'm sorry I was late again. I only just got home." The lines in his face were more pronounced than ever.

"You should have been in bed hours ago, Trace. You look exhausted. How did your meeting go?" Cassie had the hysterical urge to laugh because he'd never been in her bedroom this late at night before, and here were the two of them talking like a comfortably married couple.

"Very well, as a matter of fact, but I didn't waken you to talk about bank business. I have something much more serious on my mind."

"Is it about Lena and Allen?"

Her question seemed to baffle him. "No. Why would it be when things have never been better between them?"

"I meant to ask you about that. Why was Allen so overcome by what she said?"

"Because for all the years they've been married, Allen had a secret fear that Lena couldn't talk about her painting or even admit she was once an artist because she was still in love with her ex-lover. Allen hasn't always been the comedian he pretends to be. His jovial behavior has been a front for insecurity, even pain."

"But that's crazy!" Cassie cried. "Lena adores Allen. She's confided everything to me, and I promise you, she got over that affair years ago. She asked Allen if they could stay on in Snowbird after everyone left because she wanted to have a second honeymoon with him."

The pulse at the corner of his mouth throbbed. "Every man should be so lucky. After her unprompted confession last night, I think he's beginning to believe she loves him wholeheartedly—thanks to you."

Cassie shook her head. "Not me, Trace. You. It was your suggestion that prompted me to talk to Lena in the first place. Somehow you have a gift for making everything right for everybody. The boys are very lucky to have a father like you," she said with a catch in her voice.

"I wonder if this gift you credit me with can fix something a little closer to home."

Her heart thudded painfully at his sober tone. "What is it? What's wrong?"

A grimace marred his handsome features. "When I asked you to marry me, we agreed that if there ever came a time when we didn't like the arrangement, we'd face that problem when it arose."

It was a good thing Cassie was already in bed or she might have fainted. "I remember," she whispered, hardly able to get the words out. "I've been aware for some time that you haven't been happy. Actually I've wanted to talk to you about it, but the opportunity never seemed to present itself."

After a long pause, he said, "That's my fault. I realize I've been impossible to live with. Cassie, I can't go on this way any longer."

A numbing sickness slowly crept through her body. "You don't need to say any more. I'll move out."

To her astonishment his head reared back. "What in the hell are you talking about? I came in here tonight to tell you I hate the rules of our marriage contract and I'm asking you to start sleeping with me in my bed."

When his words sank in, Cassie felt herself go feverishly hot, then cold. She raised her eyes to him in disbelief. He muttered something unintelligible and shook his head when he saw her stunned expression.

"Living in the same house with you and not being able to make love to you has almost driven me out of my mind. Surely after the other night you can be in no

doubt about how much I want you. I almost couldn't
let you go.''

His admission opened a floodgate of emotions in
Cassie. There was no mistaking the look of desire in
his eyes as he sat down on the bed next to her and
traced the outline of her flushed face with his fingers.
''I'm aching to touch you and hold you all night long.
You're in my blood, Cassie—and I know of only one
way to solve that particular problem.''

In the next instant his mouth covered hers, forcing
her head back against the pillow. For a little while
Cassie refused to listen to her heart, which told her
there was all the difference in the world between a
man's desire for a woman and his love. The sensa-
tions his lips aroused against the tender skin of her
neck and throat were so addictive she never wanted
him to stop. She could no longer think coherently.

But when he lifted the covers to slide into bed beside her she couldn't help remembering that this was
how his son's conception had begun. By Trace's own
admission, he'd never have married Gloria if he hadn't
made her pregnant. Their passion had resulted in a
baby, but Jason wasn't the product of two people
deeply in love who needed to express those feelings in
the age-old way. They had divorced soon after the
birth.

Cassie loved Trace with a fierceness he hadn't even
guessed at. As for his feelings, she wasn't so naive that
she didn't know this would be simply another night of
physical passion for him. Sexual gratification, without the heart-deep commitment she desperately

needed. Cassie had no way of determining how many times he'd experienced this same desire for the latest woman in his life. *Because that was all she was—and she happened to be available!* The word "love" hadn't even been mentioned. When he tired of her, they'd go back to being housemates again.

Unable to tolerate that possibility, she pushed herself away from him and got to her feet. When he stood up, they faced each other from opposite sides of the narrow bed. Trace ran a hand through his already disheveled black hair, a gesture so sensual she had to close her eyes against its appeal. He would never know what denying herself his lovemaking was costing her.

"The desire seems to be all on my part."

She swallowed hard. "When two people aren't in love, then it's wrong."

The silence seemed to stretch endlessly before he said, "It's inconceivable to me that a woman as warm and beautiful and desirable as you would be willing to go through her whole life without ever experiencing sexual intimacy. I was wrong in asking you to enter this farcical arrangement."

With those words Cassie lost every vestige of hope that he might come to love her. "So far, I—I've been . . . happy with it," she stammered. "I'm sorry if it hasn't worked out for you, since you've had ample opportunity to spend your free time with anyone you wanted, no questions asked."

His features could have been cast in stone. "You're right. I have," he retorted.

"I'll move out after the opening if that's what you want."

"It's not!" he fired back, sounding more intense than she'd ever heard him before. "The boys adore you and I have living proof that they're your whole raison d'être. Any problems we have are mine and mine alone." He strode from the room without a backward glance.

Since she couldn't imagine a life without him, she should have been overjoyed that he hadn't taken her up on her offer to leave. But once he'd gone, Cassie flung herself on the bed and buried her face in the pillow to stifle her sobs.

Contrary to her expectations, for the rest of the week Trace was surprisingly kind and considerate, and never once alluded to the ugly scene in her bedroom. He came home early every night to help with the children so Cassie would be free to prepare for the opening. It reminded her of the first few weeks of their marriage, when they'd enjoyed an easy camaraderie and shared the joys of caring for the children.

But in those early days she'd still retained the hope that Trace would fall in love with her and make their marriage a real one. All she could do now was shower her affection on the children and concentrate on her business in an effort to ignore the aching void only Trace could fill.

Late Friday afternoon, before the grand opening on Saturday, Cassie was at the gallery finishing up some last-minute details when she heard a familiar voice call her name.

She spun around to face the tall, rangy man with dark brown hair and eyes who'd been watching her. "Rolfe!" Somehow in the rush of things she'd completely forgotten about his coming to Phoenix.

"You look wonderful, Cass." He held out his arms and she ran into them, hugging him tightly. "I've missed you," he murmured into her hair.

"I've missed you, too." But the way he was holding her made her realize he was about to kiss her and she quickly pulled out of his arms. "I had no idea you were in town."

"I flew in an hour ago and phoned the number Mother gave me. Your housekeeper said you were down here, so I thought I'd come and surprise you."

"You certainly did that." She smiled, then asked deliberately, "Did you bring your fiancée back with you?"

He frowned. "I thought you'd be able to tell from the telegram that I'm no longer engaged."

"And you thought you'd come back into Cassie's life and pick up where you left off?"

Cassie's eyes widened in astonishment to discover that Trace had come into the shop and was strolling toward them, still dressed in the suit he'd worn to work. He carried a sack of take-out fried chicken. She was so surprised to see him and so thrilled that he'd been thoughtful enough to bring dinner she wished Rolfe a thousand miles away.

"Trace, this is Rolfe Timpson. Rolfe, I'd like you to meet my husband, Trace Ramsey."

The two men took each other's measure, and Trace nodded, but neither put out a hand.

"What is it you're after, Timpson? My wife is busy getting ready for her opening. This isn't the best time to come calling."

Rolfe's gaze slid to Cassie's. "She knows why I'm here. Cassie and I have always belonged together. I made a mistake when I broke our engagement. I was too impatient, but I've learned my lesson and I want her back, no matter how long it takes."

"It's too late," Trace interjected before she could say anything. "Cassie's my wife now."

Undaunted, Rolfe continued to stare at her. "But I know how she really feels, and I have a letter to prove it. She married you to be close to Susan's baby, nothing more."

Dear Lord. The letter. Cassie had forgotten all about it. But that was before she'd married Trace and fallen in love with him.

Trace's body tautened. "That's right, Timpson. Now she's the mother of both my children, and that's the way it's going to stay. Have a good trip back to San Francisco." Trace put the food on the counter and darted her a mysterious glance. "I presume I'll be seeing you at home soon? Early enough to help put the boys to bed?"

"Yes," she called after him softly. "I was just closing up. Thank you for dinner." She would have kissed his cheek, but he'd already turned on his heel and walked out of the shop.

Rolfe studied her, and the silence stretched between them. "Did I misunderstand your letter, Cassie?"

She shook her head. "No. But I wrote it before I married Trace."

Again there was a long period of quiet. "You're in love with him, aren't you?"

"Yes."

He took a fortifying breath. "You were never in love with me, but I didn't want to believe it."

Cassie's eyes clouded over. "I'll always love you, Rolfe—like a brother. You're the most wonderful man I know, next to Trace."

"I threw it all away when I broke our engagement."

"No. Don't you see? If you'd really loved me the way I love Trace, you wouldn't have left. But you did because you sensed it wasn't right between us. And even if your engagement to the woman you met in Belgium didn't last, it proves you were ready for another relationship."

"I'll never forget you, Cass."

She smiled. "And I'll always remember you, because you were my first love."

CHAPTER NINE

CASSIE COULD HARDLY WAIT to get home to Trace. Maybe he wasn't in love with her, but he'd let Rolfe know in no uncertain terms that he wanted Cassie to remain his wife. It was a beginning, and she was determined that in time their marriage would become a proper one.

The minute Rolfe left the store, she closed up and sped home, snatching bites of the delicious chicken he'd brought her every time she stopped for a light.

The absence of his car in the drive sent her spirits plummeting as she pulled up to the house. And Nattie's explanation that he hadn't come home yet filled her with dread. She'd expected him to be here, playing with the children. Waiting for her.

When eleven o'clock arrived, he still hadn't come home. Cassie finally gave up her vigil and went to bed, needing sleep before her opening the next day. But it was fitful and she awakened restless and out of sorts.

The next morning after her shower, she put on a smart navy silk suit she'd purchased a few days earlier. The tailoring and sophistication bolstered her waning confidence.

Lena planned to meet her at Mix and Match at eight. Cassie went in to kiss the children goodbye before leaving for the gallery, skipping breakfast altogether. If Trace was up, she didn't see a sign of him, and she drove away from the house in tears.

"You look beautiful," Lena told her when Cassie arrived at the back entrance to the shop. "But you've been crying. What's wrong?"

"Let's go in and I'll tell you."

While they got the shop ready, Cassie explained what had happened the night before. "I don't understand him, Lena. He's like a wind that blows hot, then cold. I can't live the rest of my life this way."

"I don't like the sound of that. What are you planning to do?"

"I—I'm not sure. I have to get through today before I can make any serious decisions."

"Cassie, a word of advice. Don't act hastily. Give everything more time."

"Time seems to be making things worse."

She wasn't destined to hear Lena's response because a young man appeared at the door holding an enormous spray of the most exquisite yellow roses Cassie had ever seen. There had to be five or six dozen, at least. "I have a delivery for Cassie Ramsey."

"Oh, they're gorgeous!" Lena exclaimed. "And I have a pretty good idea who sent them."

Cassie signed for them, and when the delivery man had gone she hunted for the card tucked among the sprays of fern. "A woman like you makes her own luck, but you have all my best wishes just the same.

Trace.'' The words reminded her forcefully of another time when he'd complimented her for being able to stand on her own two feet. *Alone.*

Crushing the card in her hand, she whispered to Lena, ''Would you find a good spot for these so Trace will see them when he comes by later?''

Lena took the flowers from her. ''Heavens, Cassie. You look so pale. What's wrong?''

''Nothing. Just more of Trace's...kindness. If you'll open the machine, I'll get busy putting out the rest of the door prizes in case we have an overflow. I'm being optimistic, aren't I?'' She laughed nervously.

Lena slid a comforting arm around Cassie's waist before they both went to work. At five to ten, there were people milling around the store entrance. Her thoughts went back to a time in San Francisco when she hadn't a prayer of realizing her dream of opening a boutique. Again she had to remind herself how lucky she was. But at what price?

The next hour flew by in a blur of activity. Besides curious shoppers who lingered and raved over the displays, unable to make up their minds about what they wanted to buy, there must have been half a dozen more florist deliveries from every member of Trace's family, as well as the manager of Crossroads Square.

At eleven o'clock, another flower arrangement arrived, from Beulah no less. And right after that, three men brought in an enormous flowering cactus. A banner that wished Cassie and Lena good luck was signed, ''Compliments of the Greater Phoenix Banking Corporation.''

The noon hour brought in more traffic, and suddenly everyone seemed ready to make purchases. At one point, Cassie looked up and noted to her astonishment that the shop was slowly being denuded of its inventory. She couldn't believe it.

"Mrs. Ramsey?" someone called to her.

She turned her head and thought she recognized the manager of a well-known restaurant down the street from Crossroads Square. "I know we've met, but I'm embarrassed to say I don't remember your name."

"Hal Sykes." He grinned. "Welcome to the block. I saw your ad in the paper and decided to drop in. I'm very glad I did. There are three paintings I'm interested in purchasing, but I don't see a price on any of them. Does that mean they've already sold?"

Cassie grinned widely as she looked at Lena, madly ringing up one sale after another. "I'll tell you what," she murmured. "You can talk to the artist, Mrs. Haroldson, and see what she says. Just a minute."

With her adrenaline pumping, Cassie worked her way through the crowd to the counter. "Lena, I'll take over here. There's a Mr. Sykes standing by the cactus who wants help. He's in the pink shirt."

Lena darted him a glance. "His face looks familiar."

"That's because we ate in his restaurant the other day."

"I remember. Okay. I'll be right back."

Cassie chuckled to herself in glee when yet another customer inquired about one of the paintings and left her card. Lena didn't return until a half hour later, looking positively dazed. "What did Mr. Sykes want?" Cassie asked between sales.

Lena blinked. "He offered me five thousand dollars for the three paintings over there. He's remodeling part of his restaurant and says they'd be perfect for the decor."

Keeping a poker face, Cassie said, "I hope you told him ten thousand or nothing."

"Cassie!"

"Well?"

"I—I told him they weren't for sale, but he wrote out a check, anyway, and said he'd be back before we closed at seven, in case I changed my mind." She handed Cassie the check, made out to Mix and Match Southwest.

"I could use money like that to replenish my inventory," Cassie said matter-of-factly and put the check in the till. "Before you turn him down flat, why don't we talk about it? Say fifteen percent for every painting sold out of the store, and the rest for you?"

"Be serious," Lena said in a trembling voice.

"I am," Cassie came back. "A few minutes ago a woman told me she was interested in your sunset painting, the one with all the pinks and oranges. She's a New Yorker who wanted to take home a souvenir of Arizona. She's also an art dealer and offered four thousand for it. Here's her card. You're supposed to get in touch with her at that number next week."

"Hi, honey. How's it going?" a familiar voice broke in on their conversation.

Lena whirled around, her gray eyes luminous. "Allen!"

"I'm glad you're here." Cassie beamed at her brother-in-law. "Business is booming and we both need a break. Why don't you take your wife out for a quick lunch? When she returns, I'll grab a bite."

"Are you sure?" They both spoke at once.

"It's not quite as busy as it was earlier. But don't forget to come back. I can't run this place without you."

"A half hour," Lena promised. "No longer."

"Be sure and tell Allen about the nine thousand offered for your paintings already. And the day's only half over!"

In front of any number of interested customers, Allen let out a whoop of joy and swung Lena around before hustling her out of the shop.

Trace's clever scheme to help his sister looked as if it had succeeded, and Cassie couldn't help but take personal delight in the knowledge that she'd played a part. But with the steady stream of customers waiting to pay for their purchases, Cassie didn't have time to dwell on anything. Including the bleakness of her own future after she left Trace. . . .

There had hardly been a lull since the doors opened. Naturally the opening would attract more shoppers than Cassie could expect on a regular business day. Still, she had to admit the large turnout was gratifying, and she prayed it augured well for future sales, since she wouldn't be depending on Trace's support any longer.

While she chatted with customers and took orders for items already sold out, she was making plans to search for a small apartment in Phoenix. She could live there and still have regular access to the children. She and Trace wouldn't have to see each other; Nattie and Mike could help make visitations smooth and pleasant.

Even if Cassie felt like the boys' mother, the fact remained that she was Justin's aunt and had no blood ties to Jason whatsoever. Under the circumstances, it would be wisest to move out of Trace's home now and establish herself in the community where she could earn her living. She'd see the boys whenever possible. As long as they wanted a relationship, she would be there for them in the capacity of aunt and friend.

No matter what Trace said, in time he'd fall in love and want to marry for all the right reasons, ultimately providing the boys with a stepmother. Painful as that would be to face, Cassie knew what she had to do for the welfare of all concerned.

"Look who I brought back with me." Lena's happy voice broke in on Cassie's thoughts as she was straightening the counter. She glanced up in time to see most of Trace's family enter the shop. The Ramseys' striking looks caused heads to turn. One by one they came over to give Cassie a hug while she thanked them for the flowers.

"I'm so proud of you, dear." Olivia patted Cassie's cheek. Then nodding toward Lena, who'd taken over at the cash register, the older woman whispered, "Bless you, Cassie."

"It's Trace's doing. You know that," Cassie whispered back.

"I know a lot more than you think."

Cassie barely had time to ponder her mother-in-law's mysterious reply, because there was a commotion at the door. As she turned her head, she caught sight of a tanned, relaxed-looking Trace, wheeling in the children seated in their two-seater stroller. Their entry caused delighted outbursts from his family, as well as other shoppers who crowded round.

Trace wore chinos and a navy sports shirt, open at the neck. The boys were dressed in identical navy sailor suits she'd made for them. On their feet were spanking white shoes and socks. They looked so marvelous Cassie forgot where she was and could do nothing more than lean against the glass countertop for support, feasting her eyes. There they were, not ten feet away. The three people in the world she loved more than life itself.

At that moment she experienced a pain so staggering she thought she might faint. Since the children hadn't yet seen her, she said, "Lena, excuse me for a minute." Without waiting to hear her sister-in-law's reply, Cassie hurried to the back room, which served as a supply area with an adjoining bathroom.

She waited until the wave of sickness had passed, then applied fresh lipstick before going back out. Trace was waiting for her on the other side of the door, his face alarmed. He put a hand to her forehead. "I saw you dash in here. You're white as parchment. Are you sick?"

Cassie took a deep breath. "No. It's probably a combination of nerves and the fact that we've been so busy all day I haven't had a chance to eat yet."

A pulse throbbed at his temple as he ushered her to a utility chair and forced her to sit down. "Then let's get you something right now. Lena said she'd be fine and Mother's watching the children."

"Actually, I don't feel like going anyplace, but a drink would be wonderful. There's a grocery farther down in the mall."

"Stay here and I'll get it." He was gone in a flash and returned not only with a carton of milk but an apple. Cassie thanked him and proceeded to enjoy both.

"The color's returned to your cheeks," he murmured after she'd finished the milk.

"I feel fine now, and a bit of a fool. Thank you for coming to my rescue. I should've packed a lunch and brought it with me, but I never dreamed there'd be so many customers."

He studied her face for a long moment. "I told the boys their mother's shop would be a raving success. They wanted to see for themselves, and so did I." He paused, still watching her closely. "I hope you don't mind."

Cassie jumped up from the chair and averted her eyes to hide the turmoil going on inside her. Did he mean what he was implying, or was this another ploy to convince the family they were a happily married couple?

"Of course I don't mind. I'm thrilled to see them. They look adorable in those outfits, don't they? Let's go find them."

Trace put a detaining hand on her arm. "Are you sure you're feeling all right?"

"Of course. I just needed a pick-me-up. Thank you."

Too affected by his nearness, Cassie hurried out front with Trace at her heels and discovered the boys being held by James and Norman. The minute the children saw Cassie they squealed in excitement and wriggled in their uncles' arms, trying to reach her.

With patrons in the store to wait on, she couldn't do more than kiss the children. They started crying when she left them to walk behind the counter.

"I'll get them out of here before we disrupt things any more," Trace offered.

"The flowers are beautiful. Thank you for making all this possible. And for coming."

She heard his quick intake of breath. "I'm your husband, for heaven's sake. Why wouldn't I be here?" he muttered angrily. She dared a brief glance at him and thought she detected a flash of pain in the blue eyes that bore into hers. He fairly bristled with emotion as he turned swiftly to gather the children. Cassie wanted to call him back, but now was not the time.

For the rest of the day she was haunted by the look in Trace's eyes, and she simply went through the motions as she greeted customers and rang up sales. By six-thirty the crowds had diminished; for the first time all day Cassie and Lena were able to straighten the remaining merchandise and start ringing out the cash register.

"All the Southwest pieces sold," Cassie commented in surprise. Automatically her eyes sought out the painting that had first inspired them, but it wasn't there. She frowned. "Lena? Where's your Hopi girl painting?"

Her sister-in-law blushed. "Would you believe Allen bought it and took it home with him? He left a check in the register."

"Good for him," she murmured. "Trace thinks it's your best painting and I agree with him. Lena, would you mind very much closing up for me tonight? I have something I need to do."

"I might as well start now, since I'm going to need the practice." Cassie's head lifted in query. "You might as well know. I've been painting again and I've been having the time of my life. Allen and I talked about it over lunch. If your offer is still open, I'd like to be the other half of this business venture."

Wordlessly Cassie flung her arms around Lena's slender shoulders and hugged her.

"Allen's coming any minute and we'll take care of everything. Go home to Trace," Lena urged.

"That's what I'm going to do. I love him and I'm going to tell him exactly how I feel. No matter what his response is, I can't hide my emotions any longer."

But when she returned to the house, it was still and dark. The children were gone. Not even Nattie and Mike were around. In a state of panic, Cassie phoned the shop and cried out in relief when Lena answered.

"Lena, it's Cassie. There's no one home, not even the children. Do you have any idea where Trace might have gone with them?"

"I think I heard Mom offer to take the boys overnight."

"Thanks. I'll call over there." Sure enough, Olivia Ramsey was baby-sitting and told Cassie that Trace had said something about working late at the office. Cassie thanked her and hung up the phone, a plan already forming in her mind.

She ran to her workroom closet and retrieved the six-foot alligator hidden behind the material. After stuffing it into the car, she sped along the highway toward the heart of Phoenix. Nighttime traffic was moderate, so she made it downtown within half an hour. Fortunately, the parking lot, almost empty now, stayed lighted all night long. As she drove in, she immediately saw Trace's black Mercedes, and she pulled up next to it, her heart hammering almost painfully.

The alligator made an awkward burden but she managed to half-carry, half-drag it to the security guard's cubicle. He had no idea who she was, since she'd been in the bank only once before. It seemed a century ago to Cassie.

He stared at the alligator, then at her, his eyes narrowing suspiciously. "Can I help you, ma'am?"

"My husband is here working late. I decided to surprise him."

He looped his thumbs over his belt, drawing her attention to his hip holster. "The only person in the building is Mr. Ramsey."

"I'm Mrs. Ramsey. We've never met." She put out her hand but he didn't shake it. Cassie's mood bordered on hysteria—why was she barred from seeing her own husband?

"I'll have to call and let him know you're down here."

"But that would spoil my surprise." She tried to appear friendly as she said it, hoping to win him over. But the man remained adamant.

"Sorry. I can't let you in without his okay."

She bit her lip in frustration and searched in her handbag for her wallet. "Here." She thrust her credit cards and driver's license at him.

He glanced at them, then shook his head.

She sighed angrily. "Then you leave me no choice. Will you please let him know Cassie would like to see him?"

The sandy-haired man nodded and picked up the phone. "Mr. Ramsey? There's a woman down here who claims to be your wife. She says her name's Cassie and she has ID to that effect—but you never know..."

Cassie tapped her foot impatiently as the guard gave her the once-over.

"She's about five two or three, blond, green-eyed. She's also good looking—and, uh, built, if you know what I mean," he murmured in a lowered voice, but Cassie heard him and felt heat rush to her face. "The thing is, she's carrying this stuffed animal around that's bigger than she is," he confided. "Yes, sir." He nodded, then turned to Cassie. "Can I see that thing, ma'am?" he asked unexpectedly.

"Be my guest," she muttered, wishing she could throw it at him.

Putting down the phone, he grabbed the alligator and looked it up and down, then examined it front and back, before picking up the receiver again. "It's a green 'gator about six feet in length with black hair, blue eyes and a wicked grin. It says 'Daddy' on the tail." He laughed as he spoke. After another moment, he said, "Yes, *sir!*" and hung up. All signs of mirth had vanished.

"*Now* do I have your permission to go up?" she asked in her iciest tone. Enough was enough!

"Sorry, ma'am. I can't let you do that." After propping the alligator against the glass, he reached for his belt, and before she knew what had happened, he had fastened something metal around her wrist. She was so astonished she'd actually stood there and let him handcuff her to his wrist.

"Now, wait just a minute!" she raged, trying to pull away from him, thinking it had to be a trick. But she might as well have saved her energy.

"It seems a woman bearing your description barged into his office a few months ago with some outrageous story. He said if you were the one, you could be dangerous. He told me to detain you until he comes down and checks you out. I'm only doing my job, ma'am."

"Which you do admirably, Lewis."

Furious, Cassie turned in the direction of her husband's voice. He stepped out of the elevator, his black hair attractively mussed, still wearing the casual navy outfit he'd had on earlier. Without giving her as much as a glance, he reached for the alligator and studied it thoroughly.

"She's the one, Lewis. Unlock the handcuffs and I'll take her upstairs. I want an unofficial statement from her before she goes anywhere."

"Yes, sir!"

Firmly gripping her elbow with one hand and clutching the alligator under his other arm, he guided her into the elevator. "By the way, Lewis," Trace offered before the doors closed, "she *is* my wife, but don't let anyone else know she's been running around loose on the premises carrying this monster."

The elevator began its ascent. "And now, Mrs. Ramsey..." Trace backed her into a corner, trapping her with his powerful body and the green felt alligator. "You have exactly ten seconds to explain yourself. I'm counting."

He looked and sounded every bit as forbidding as he had that first day in his office. But this time, she wasn't planning to reason with him. Nor was she going to bait him.

"I'm in love with you," she admitted simply.

"Since when?" he retorted with lips tantalizingly close to hers. The elevator doors opened and he urged her out, but she was barely aware of her surroundings.

"Since the moment you first accused me of being part of a kidnapping scheme, she whispered."

His left brow dipped in displeasure, just like Jason's always did. "Don't lie to me, Cassie."

"I'm not. I swear it!" she cried. "In spite of everything, I felt this overwhelming attraction to you and I knew from your reaction how much you adored Justin. I began to realize then that I'd met the man I wanted to live with for the rest of my life."

She felt his body tauten. "Why didn't you admit it when I took you to Snowbird, or the other night when I was begging you to sleep with me?"

"Because I didn't think you loved me! You never told me you did."

He groaned, shaking his head impatiently. "Because I didn't want to scare you off after that absurd marriage contract I'd made with you. Don't you know I fell in love with you the second you raced across the office to comfort my howling, black-haired son? I thought if I could ever get you to love *me* that fiercely, I'd be the happiest man alive."

"Trace..." She reached up to cover his mouth with her own, revealing the burning intensity of her need, realizing that this was what they'd both been hungering for from the very beginning. One day soon she'd tell him about her talk with Rolfe. But not right now.

Right now... She moaned in ecstasy at the way Trace was making her feel, the things he was doing to her with his hands and mouth.

"Do you have any idea the kind of hell I've been going through, waiting for Rolfe to show up, terrified you'd decide to go back to him?"

"I have an idea, yes," she said softly, pressing hot kisses against his eyes and lips. "All this time I've been afraid you wanted to make love to me because it was convenient, that eventually you'd grow tired of me and I'd end up being ex-wife number two."

"Never!" He kissed her long and hard. "I should have told you how I felt when I came to your apartment in San Francisco. But I was afraid to admit the truth—it seemed too soon to be feeling like that. We barely knew each other. And after that fiery scene at the airport, I couldn't risk losing you, so I had to come up with a foolproof plan to make you fall in love with me."

She traced his mouth with her fingertips. "And you succeeded. To be your wife, even if it was in name only, brought me more happiness than you can possibly imagine. I knew then that my feelings for Rolfe weren't the kind a woman has to have for the man she marries. I love you, darling. Only you. Forever."

"I've waited to hear those words for so long," he whispered against her lips. Then he started to kiss her with passionate urgency, bringing to life every nerve ending in her body. The world reeled away as Trace picked her up in his arms. Ignoring the alligator, he carried her into a room she hadn't seen before. It looked more like the interior of an elegant hotel.

"This isn't part of your office, is it?" she asked, trying to catch her breath when she saw the photograph she'd given him hanging on the wall.

Trace favored her with a voluptuous smile. "We're about to begin our honeymoon in my penthouse suite."

Cassie blinked. "I didn't even know you had one. Is this where you stayed on the nights you weren't at the house?"

"That's right." He carried her to the big picture window, which looked out over the city of Phoenix. "I've spent hours standing here, gazing in the direction of our house, wondering if you ever lay awake nights wanting me, aching for me the way I did you."

Cassie pulled his head down and moved her lips sensuously against his. "Let's go to bed and I'll show you what it's been like for me."

She blushed at his appreciative chuckle and hid her face in his shoulder. "To think Jason brought me here... to this..."

"Cassie!" He tightened his arms around her. "What if you'd given up your search too soon?"

"But I didn't." She bit delicately on his earlobe, producing a groan that vibrated through her body. "Susan wanted Jason to be united with his real father, and I wanted that, too."

He pressed her closer still. "I love your sister for that. I love our sons, but above all, I love you, Cassie. I need you in all the ways a man needs his wife. Don't ever stop loving me."

His vulnerability was a revelation to her. "Why do you think I agreed to your scheme to open a shop for Lena's sake? I planned to be so well and truly tied to you you'd never be able to get rid of me."

A deep, happy laugh came out of Trace as he moved them toward the bed. "My adorable wife, much as I love my sister, *you* were the real reason I thought up that scheme. I hoped it would fulfill you so much you'd never leave me. I threw in Lena's problems to win your sympathy, hoping but never dreaming she'd actually go along with it."

Cassie had never known this kind of joy before. She sought his mouth again and again, craving the feel and taste of him. "Then you got more than you bargained for, because tonight she informed me she wants half interest in the business. Apparently she's started painting again."

She felt his fingers tighten in her curls. "I know. Allen confided as much to me earlier today. He's anxious to talk to you and thank you for helping strengthen their marriage. But I told him he'd have a long wait because I had plans of my own where you were concerned."

"I'm glad you said that," she murmured. "You're right—Jason and Justin are entirely too spoiled. Another baby would be good for them—and for me. How about you?"

His smile slowly faded, to be replaced by a look of such burning sensuality she trembled in his arms. "I'm prepared to indulge your desires indefinitely, Mrs. Ramsey."

HARLEQUIN ROMANCE®

IF YOU THOUGHT ROMANCE NOVELS WERE ALL THE SAME...LOOK AGAIN!

Our new look begins this September

Harlequin Romance has a fresh new cover that's sure to catch your eye—and our warm, contemporary love stories are sure to touch your heart!

Watch for a sneak preview of our new covers next month!

HARLEQUIN ROMANCE—
A lifetime of love

HRT

HARLEQUIN
Romance

**HARLEQUIN ROMANCE
IS IN THE
WEDDING BUSINESS...**

The August title in The Bridal Collection is
about...a wedding consultant!

**THE BEST-MADE PLANS
by Leigh Michaels**

THE BRIDAL COLLECTION

THE BRIDE arranged weddings.
The Groom avoided them.
Their own Wedding was ten years late!

Available wherever
Harlequin books are sold.

WED-4A

WELCOME TO

The quintessential small town where everyone knows everybody else!

Finally, books that capture the pleasure of tuning in to your favorite TV show!

GREAT READING... GREAT SAVINGS... AND A FABULOUS FREE GIFT!

Each book set in Tyler is a self-contained love story; together, the twelve novels stitch the fabric of the community. The covers honor the old American tradition of quilting; each cover depicts a patch of the large Tyler quilt.

With Tyler you can receive a fabulous gift ABSOLUTELY FREE by collecting proofs-of-purchase found in each Tyler book. And use our special Tyler coupons to save on your next TYLER book purchase.

Join your friends at Tyler for the sixth book, SUNSHINE by Pat Warren, available in August.

When Janice Eber becomes a widow, does her husband's friend David provide more than just friendship?

If you missed *Whirlwind* (March), *Bright Hopes* (April), *Wisconsin Wedding* (May), *Monkey Wrench* (June) or *Blazing Star* (July) and would like to order them, send your name, address, zip or postal code, along with a check or money order for $3.99 (please do not send cash), plus 75¢ postage and handling ($1.00 in Canada) for each book ordered, payable to Harlequin Reader Service to:

In the U.S.

3010 Walden Avenue
P.O. Box 1325
Buffalo, NY 14269-1325

In Canada

P.O. Box 609
Fort Erie, Ontario
L2A 5X3

Please specify book title(s) with your order.
Canadian residents add applicable federal and provincial taxes.

TYLER-6

JAYNE ANN KRENTZ

Dreams
Parts One & Two

The warrior died at her feet, his blood running out of the cave entrance and mingling with the waterfall. With his last breath he cursed the woman—told her that her spirit would remain chained in the cave forever until a child was created and born there....

So goes the ancient legend of the Chained Lady and the curse that bound her throughout the ages—until destiny brought Diana Prentice and Colby Savager together under the influence of forces beyond their understanding. Suddenly they were both haunted by dreams that linked past and present, while their waking hours were filled with danger. Only when Colby, Diana's modern-day warrior, learned to love, could those dark forces be vanquished. Only then could Diana set the Chained Lady free....